MIND
CAPSULE

By Jack W. Chalmers

Order this book online at www.trafford.com
or email orders@trafford.com

Most Trafford titles are also available at major online book retailers.

Cover and Illustrations by Jack W. Chalmers.
Email: cwleod@shaw.ca

Note for Librarians: A cataloguing record for this book is available from Library and Archives Canada at www.collectionscanada.ca/amicus/index-e.html

Printed in Victoria, BC, Canada.

ISBN: 978-1-4251-8415-5 (sc)

We at Trafford believe that it is the responsibility of us all, as both individuals and corporations, to make choices that are environmentally and socially sound. You, in turn, are supporting this responsible conduct each time you purchase a Trafford book, or make use of our publishing services. To find out how you are helping, please visit www.trafford.com/responsiblepublishing.html

Our mission is to efficiently provide the world's finest, most comprehensive book publishing service, enabling every author to experience success. To find out how to publish your book, your way, and have it available worldwide, visit us online at www.trafford.com

Trafford rev. 7/14/2009

www.trafford.com

North America & International
toll-free: 1 888 232 4444 (USA & Canada)
phone: 250 383 6864 ♦ fax: 250 383 6804
email: info@trafford.com

CONTENTS

DISCOVERY

THERE IT SAT, protruding from the dry soil, just as Boyd said: a thick copper dome over three meters in diameter, corroded and pitted from the ravages of age. Doctor Niemeyer knew the find must have been extraordinary by the tone of the telegram he received, but he thought a mummy, a celestial calendar, nothing so colossal, so absolutely confirming of his theory if it all checked out to be what he dared believe.

From the ridge of debris he could see a porthole. Despite his sixty-five years he lost no time in scrambling into the excavation pit, and resting his thin frame against the shell, thrust his head into the opening.

A mellow green light bathed the inside of the strange metal bubble, eliminating all interior shadow. An oblong block of indiscernible substance protruded from a flat, metallic floor, placed off center to allow movement under the curved roof. Strange inscriptions surrounded its base, like none the doctor had ever seen. From the block radiated strayed patterns along the floor, that evolved into convolutions of copper spreading up the curved walls. Despite the evident technology, the whole construction was immaculately simple.

How old was the shell? How long had it lain with its silent secrets? If he was correct, it was older than the pyramids.

"This definitely confirms your theory," said a blond, crew cut youth from a distance behind him. "It's what we've been looking for."

"Let's not jump to conclusions, Sidney." He tore his gaze from the porthole and worked his way back to Sidney Boyd, who had remained standing on the excavation rubble. "We can't say this dome has any historical significance until we determine its age. Judging from the exterior corrosion, though, I would say it's incredibly old."

Another associate, unknown to the doctor, was leaning with his back against their rented jeep, stuffing tobacco into an oversized pipe. "You know, Doctor," the stranger said, "I could swear before that porthole opened there wasn't the slightest cut in that metal. I don't mean just a very close fit. I mean nothing, as if there had never been a cut there."

"Ah! You must be Mister Ryan. I understand it was you who made this find."

"He's the one, Doctor," Boyd interjected. "Charlie's had a keen interest in your views for years. A real idea man too. You'll find him a valuable addition to our team."

The doctor and Ryan exchanged cordialities. "Your observation is certainly strange...incredible, in fact. But first tell me how you found this dome."

The request was badly timed for Charlie Ryan had begun lighting his beloved pipe. He gave great heaves to finish the task, then replaced the lighter in his vest pocket. Ryan was heavy set, bald except for a short fringe of greying hair at ear level, and sported a beaked nose that protruded from an otherwise unimpressive face. He took several drags before settling into a short chat: "As you see, Doctor, the region here is quite open, giving us a view of mounds that might arouse our suspicion. We've been looking around this desert for about five weeks, isn't that right, Sidney?"

Boyd nodded agreement.

"Our method of search has been to scout the countryside

to stick probes into mounds that look promising, then decide whether or not to excavate since our funds are so limited we can't dig up everything we'd like. Well, I came across this mound and when I put my few Bolivian hands to work clearing off its top layers of dirt, lo and behold, what emerged was that dome."

Ryan paused to replace the curved pipe between his yellow teeth, releasing a puff of smoke that leisurely dissipated in the cool air of the altiplano. "I immediately set my help clearing away every speck of dirt over the find, and what they uncovered were three square indentures arranged in a ninety degree triangle, like Pythagoras' Theorem. When I tapped them they..." he looked up at Niemeyer soberly, choosing his words carefully, "...glowed momentarily, very dimly but enough that I could just make out their light. Their arrangement gave me the idea of tapping them in Pythagoras' relationship, three, four, five, because their squares add: nine plus sixteen equals twenty-five. Three taps for the small square, four for the next and five for the hypotenuse square. It was just a guess. When I finished, a circular crack appeared in the metal and the whole portion blew in. That's what gave the porthole you were just looking into."

The doctor peered at Ryan through thick, frameless glasses, his face flushed and jaw sagged open under his bushy moustache. Ryan obviously expected his account to be received with skepticism, but with the green glow emanating from the dome even now as he looked at it, Doctor Niemeyer didn't know how anyone could find it far-fetched. On the contrary, the more he learned of the dome the more amazed he became. Could it be something other than an artefact left by ancient people?

He did not have long to ponder the question as his attention was diverted by two figures, of a youthful man and woman, running from a near-by camp. On their approach the doctor was immediately swept into the jubilance of broad smiles and aggressive hand-shaking.

"Leslie and Mark Jennings," Boyd said, introducing them. "They arrived today from work at Tiahuanaco. They're very interested in your theory on history."

College people, thought the doctor. At least his ideas had some circulation among the younger generation. That was some consolation for his years of hard work. Bringing the attention of everyone again to the dome: "I suppose you think it's a tomb."

Boyd nodded affirmatively.

"Our first job is to open the rectangular object inside, whatever it is; perhaps a kind of coffin...a 'sarcophagus'," he added, waiving his hand airily, knowing the word did not exactly fit. "Have you tried?"

Ryan answered: "No. We thought it was best to leave everything until you arrived." He paused, with narrowed eyes. "You know, I believe the dome couldn't possibly be a tomb. It's true that tombs are sometimes opened for ceremonial purposes, but this shell was designed to be opened."

"You believe it might be an attempt to communicate with the future?"

"Not only that," Ryan tore the pipe from his mouth and poked the air with its stub, at the doctor, "it could be an attempt to communicate only with people possessing a degree of technical sophistication. That's the reason for the Pythagorean puzzle. It would be a freak accident if someone opened that porthole who didn't have some knowledge of Mathematics. Perhaps it was meant for a king or some other potentate who would have access to educated servants. They probably couldn't imagine it being opened by some ordinary, retired engineer like

me. But really, I do believe there's a message in this shell. All
we have to do is learn to read it."

The doctor gazed back at Ryan. A twisted brow deformed
his thin face. "Whatever it is, it's fairly empty. I suspect it has
been pillaged..."

"Not at all!" Ryan responded. "A partial vacuum caused
that porthole to blow in. I'm convinced the shell is as intact as
the day it was sealed. It contains information its constructors
thought too important to give to a non-scientific people." He
again jabbed the air with the stub of his pipe. "They wanted
some assurance its message wouldn't be passed on as legend,
drowned in superstition."

The thought of a direct link with the past, a time capsule,
caused Doctor Niemeyer's eyes to open wide, to stare excitedly, wonderingly, quizzically. He paced back and forth over
the dry soil, head lowered, hands locked behind his back. A
time capsule would contain objects from one age to give to another, but how could a nearly empty shell fulfill that purpose if
Ryan was correct? "Most strange, most strange," he mumbled,
then stopped his ambling: "Why this shape, one of the hard-
est shapes to construct, and why made of copper? Why not
use stone, like so many other structures we see from Andean
civilization?"

"That puzzled me too, Doctor. Of course, the spherical
shape gives structural strength to a soft metal, but it still doesn't
explain why copper was used in the first place. I think copper
has another property we shouldn't overlook: its electrical conductivity, strange as that may seem for a device this old."

"It's mind boggling," Boyd interrupted. "But you might be
on to something, Charlie. There's obviously a power source for
that interior light."

"Yes, but I don't mean for lighting. I think the copper could be a shield. Against what? I don't know. The shell was obviously built to protect the 'sarcophagus' and the electrical properties of copper might add to that protection. It's just another idea we should keep in mind."

The day had already grown late and a red sky hung over the western horizon. Boyd suggested: "Let's continue our thoughts about this at camp. It'll soon be dark."

They agreed there was nothing else to accomplish that day. Their work would resume in earnest early next morning. After securing a tarpaulin over the dome, they left the site.

Everyone retired early that evening in preparation for the morning, but as the hours ticked by, Doctor Niemeyer found he could not sleep. He lay on his cot with his hands folded beneath his head, gazing up in the blackness at the ceiling of Boyd's tent, unable to wrench his mind off the events of the afternoon and their significance to him personally. For thirteen years he compiled an extensive list of historical oddities in an effort to prove the existence of a highly developed culture in the distant past, that continued to affect Earth's history long after its disappearance. He knew that legends of 'lost continents' were mythical, yet there was a period when the sciences were advanced much further than modern scholars realized. Those ancient people, whoever they were, passed their learning to the barbarians who developed the civilizations we know. In every case where civilization arose, crude and ignorant peoples emerged from jungles and wilderness with a high degree of technical knowledge, producing accomplishments in massive stone that baffle engineers even today. In every case, the more magnificent structures were built in the *beginning* of their respective civilizations, not after centuries of technical development. Egypt's pyramids were built during the Old Kingdom, not the later Empire, and architectural development from the earliest stone masonry to the Great Pyramid of Khufu lasted no more than a hundred and twenty-five years. The pattern was the same everywhere, throughout the ages.

But if ancient technology wasn't sufficiently convincing, cultural similarities spread over the globe were another thread in his weave of proof. Similar artistic styles were evident between the Maya and Chinese, and the Mayan calendar resembled the Balinese. In both Old and New Worlds people played similar games and musical instruments, danced similar dances, had similar legends like the Flood, and erected stepped mounds, pyramids, pagodas and temples. All the evidence pointed solely to one conclusion: somewhere, long ago, there existed a culture highly developed in scientific thought, that distributed its benefits to the civilizations of history. The whole of Earth's past was connected. A common inheritance ran through it all.

Try as he had, with all his amassed facts, he could not enlist the co-operation, or even the friendly endorsement of his views, of any respectable scientist. Whenever he attempted to prove his theory amid the halls of higher learning he was met with amused silence. He made requests from foundations the world over for financial assistance, spoke at universities in every country of the industrialized world, spent his own time and resources on archaeological 'digs'. In the end he only succeeded in making himself look ridiculous to the learned elite, and was able to convince only a limited few, amateurs like Sidney Boyd and Charlie Ryan, who were fired with enough dedication to make up for legions, but were not professionals in the field of archaeology.

In that year of 1959, after years of research, his case narrowed to South America and to the Bolivian plateau. *Now*, he was certain, the tables had turned. The copper dome somehow held proof that he was correct. The most intransigent faculty member of the most conservative university would have to be convinced. He, Samuel P. Niemeyer, would be hailed as a new Schliemann! But in what way could the almost empty shell hold any secrets? Obviously the answer was in the interior 'sarcophagus'.

The doctor tossed on his cot. Finally he rose, deciding he would never sleep that night. From the opposite side of the tent he could hear the even breathing of Sidney Boyd. *Good, he thought, Boyd is asleep.* He felt for his glasses, found them, then switched on a flashlight to scan his quarters. In the corner of the tent was a small table supporting a kerosene lamp and dirty coffee cup. His clothes were draped over a chair next to the table. Hastily he put on his trousers, heavy shirt, boots, jacket and cap, then quietly eased himself out of the tent. He was going back, alone, to the site.

A moment of doubt rushed over Doctor Niemeyer as he stood in the still darkness; or was it fear to face the unknown? He approached the dome apprehensively, peeled back the tarpaulin and again peered into the mellow interior. Its green luminance ran over his face and shoulders, etching him against the blackness of the star-lit sky. He raised himself on the corroded surface and shoved one leg through the porthole, then supporting his weight from his shoulders, lowered himself through the opening and fell to the side of the peculiar, box-like 'sarcophagus'. He could then clearly see the inscriptions surrounding its base, and knew they were unrelated to any known culture. He examined the puzzling structure...not glass, not plastic, not like any material he had ever seen. The whole sophistication of the find, including its radiance, emphasized a technology completely unfamiliar. A slow realization percolated in his mind, one he had already speculated upon when listening to Ryan's account but did not dare put into words. He firmly believed the ancients were more advanced than historians realized, but they could not have been *this* advanced. *No, he thought, ancient people did not make this marvel.* But if they did not, who did? There was only one answer: *It came from elsewhere, from some place other than Earth!*

The beat of his heart was strong in his ears, hairs bristled on his neck, every instinct demanded that he run. His eyes turned automatically up to the porthole. It was still open. The dome was not a trap. Slowly his old composure returned. He was a scientist dedicated to the pursuit of knowledge, even if he had to put his life on the line. Here within his grasp was everything he wanted to know, here was the vindication of his theory, his momentous chance to absolve himself from scientific heresy. He wasn't going to throw that away in an instant of panic. Somehow he had to unlock the secret of that pristine block imposing its presence in that circular chamber.

A bead of cold sweat trickled down his face as he stared at what he then knew with certainty to be a 'sarcophagus', but of a type he never thought possible. As the blue light beginning to shine inside its translucent structure transfixed his eyes, he could clearly see motion within: swirls of cloud passing through a radiant crystal. The 'sarcophagus' seemed to be coming to life, advertising its intent telepathically. Inside, a circular device materialized, that grew from an interior cloud drifting to the surface. A haze distorted the object as it emerged from the crystal, and when cleared he saw, sitting on the hard surface which only moments before had all appearances of a liquid, a large ring.

The peculiar oval was of pure silver and not completely closed. Across the opening was a small disc suspended by two fine fibres. The shape of the ring suggested a tiara. After a thoughtful moment he placed it on his head, and immediately heightened perception exploded in his brain. Billions of cells electrified into fervent activity. His lethargic body seemed to be floating. Time was speeded up. His mind was racing. The 'sarcophagus' then made sense to him. It *was* a doorway to the past.

The dome *was* a time capsule, but its constructors were not content merely to leave the trinkets of their world as amusements to people of the future. Those people of the future were to visit them, live as they once lived, see, feel and smell the sights which they had, to discover their ancient world in its entirety. All this was open to the doctor, a highway into time beckoned, and as he gazed into the swirls he felt himself drawn inside, the blue light and swirls encompassing his entire being. Bodily control drained away, in a sense of detachment, not paralysis. His mind and body were no longer joined in a single entity, his mind was floating through space, adrift on a sea of eternity, and everywhere were the swirls that grew heavier, that gradually extinguished all consciousness.

Doctor Niemeyer awoke as if from a troubled dream, with a strange sense of age in his limbs. Gradually his clouded mind discerned the old man standing directly in front of him, a man who appeared in his eighties, with white hair and beard, bright eyes only slightly faded from so many years, and faintly stooped shoulders that still hinted at a robust frame in its youth. His clothes were of a style completely unknown, the man being dressed in a sleeved tunic tied at the waist, with a wide sash that trailed down a pleated skirt. His legs were clothed by pants pulled tight at the knees, and on his feet and shins were shinning, tight windings. His whole appearance was one of elegance and importance. Most noticeable of his attire was a silver tiara that held a small disc pressed between his eyes.

Greetings to the past.

Did the old man speak? Not a trace of movement was evident on his lips.

Through the technology of my time you and I, future one, have become the same in mind. My thoughts and emotions are yours, and shortly the most salient portions of my life will be yours as well. My intentions are to give you the occurrences of my life as if you lived them, in the hope of conveying to the future that which has transpired. In them you will learn of a great danger that threatens your world.

First, I shall demonstrate. I raise a small hammer and bring it down swiftly before me. There is the smash and tinkle of broken glass. The image of an old man you had before you has disappeared in the crash, and what you see now is the opposite side of this stone room between jagged edges of broken mirror. **The old man is you!** *My mind and body have become your mind and body. Thus it is that I can speak to you without uttering vocal sounds, without knowing your language, and this over a time span of thousands of years.* **We are one!**

I am Lucirin, developed twenty-ninth year of the cycle Andranaudae, rebel Aesir. I am of the same flesh as you, a descendant of Earth, without belonging here. I came into existence in a far-off world. 'Born' is not the proper word for people like me. You may think it strange that people do not have to be born, depending on the level of your science. It matters little. All will be explained shortly. We shall first return to the world of my youth, and from there follow the events of my life consecutively. You will live through them in my person.

The device that enables me to do this is the 'sarcophagus' with which you are already familiar. It is a memory transcriber, capable of many wondrous duties, but for my purpose will serve as a thought storage and transfer machine. I assume you are technically sophisticated, but since I cannot take for granted that your knowledge is equal to mine I must explain that a person's brain has recorded in its cells every detail of his or her life. Although you may think memories of minor occurrences are lost, a smell, for example, associated with a remote happening, they are not, so a reoccurrence of that same smell much later in life may trigger a whole chain of memories that were thought long forgotten. The cerebral processes do occasionally reroute existing neural pathways to make way for new information; nevertheless, most experiences are retained by the brain in a way that allows for detailed reconstruction. Every experience is retained by the brain in minute detail, that simply needs reawakening.

I have already synchronized the transcriber with my life history. It will search my brain for memories corresponding to periods in my life I have selected, stimulate my memory into a very realistic dream, and record the memory. That memory will then last in a dormant state for millennia, to be passed on to the next person who uses the transcriber. You, of course, are that person, and my memories will be as real to you as they are to me, although thousands of years of this planet will have passed between us. Again I shall live the life of younger times, journey between the stars, visit worlds with strange happenings. And you will be there. In the end you will have lived two lives, your own and mine - mine that has ended millennia before your existence.

Although I have been rich and powerful in life it is the memories of my life that are all I have left to give. Pay careful attention to them, future one, learn well by them, for they speak of a great danger to your world. Take this knowledge and warn the people of your time, for it is a danger that is world encompassing. If you fail, a curse will descend upon all future generations of Earth, a curse as inevitable as night following day, as implacable as ice over an arctic sea.

I shall begin. I prostrate myself upon the transcriber. A billion particles vibrate beneath. My body loosens its grip upon my mind and I begin to float in the timeless swirl. The machine searches my mind. The world becomes dark, I am losing consciousness... Already I sense the strength and vigor of ...my youth...

2

THE LECTURE

"DREAMING AGAIN, LUCIRIN?" the girl sitting next to me asks.

"What? Oh, yes..." Leaning back from my sitting position, I support myself with arms behind to view the soaring artwork. "Look at this place, Maiori. It's fabulous. Have you seen it before?"

Brilliant sunlight streams from a cupola high above, reflecting from fractal patterns through lenses and mirrors to stone lace-work and elaborate decor worked into granite columns. The effect is airy, regardless of the massive structure.

"Never. It's such a privilege."

"The number of benches confirms that ... mostly empty." A scouting glance around the immense room verifies my remark. We form a small cluster of students seated near a speaking arena. "That's selection for you. Why are we here? Any idea?"

"To have our origins explained by lecture. It's a welcomed break from our usual studies, don't you think? The memory transcribers are tiring. Today's lesson must really be special."

The light from above makes a nimbus effect in Maiori's hair. It ripples across her white, silken tunic. At times like this, sitting next to her, I would prefer if we were alone.

The excited murmur of the students subsides as a heavy curtain at a side wall parts. A commanding figure moves swiftly into the speaking arena, a woman of importance, a Veradi, one of the priest-rulers of our world, Aesiris.

"I wish a cheerful morning to you young Aesir," she begins.

"I am Mayfis, and it is my purpose this morning to instruct you on Origins. I know this is a topic which has interested you for a long time, since you all seem aware that our flesh is not native to Aesiris."

Mayfis is lean and erect. Her head is clean shaven, as is the custom with the Veradi. She has a high forehead, piercing eyes, sharp nose and stern mouth. There is not a wrinkle on her face that would portray joy or sorrow. Her whole personage suggests someone under the strictest self-control, who could, and would, endure the greatest hardship in service of the Belief.

Wasting no time she immediately swings into her lecture: "Our primitive origins were on a world in a remote region of the galaxy. I'm sure you have all heard of the Tsia, and perhaps you thought of them as mythical beings, but they were... are...very real, and it is due to them that we are established on Aesiris."

Mayfis warms up to her subject. She places her hands into the oversized cuffs of her tunic, and regardless of her stoic exterior is inwardly enjoying lecturing. The subject is without doubt one of particular interest to her.

"Although our origins on Aesiris are intimately bound with the Tsia, not much is known about their origins except that they came from a world very far away, in a remote corner of the galaxy that they left eons ago. We know from the sacred writings that their world was very advanced technically, but like all worlds not in possession of true enlightenment, its society failed."

Mayfis bows her head and begins to pace back and forth in the debating arena. The thought of a society's failure apparently weighs heavily on her.

"Now I would like to digress for a moment to discuss how

this could be. How does any society fail, especially one as advanced as that of the Tsia?"

A number of hands rise from the students.

"Alright, Usla, I'll pick you. What is your understanding of why societies fail?"

The student Usla rises from the group. Unlike most Aesir, Usla possesses a pudgy frame, which I judge to be the cause of his obvious insecurity and a less obvious but nauseating obsequiousness to authority. Afflicted with an eye twitch that progresses with his emotional state, in the excitement of being called upon it twitches.

"It must be due to the Law of Random Regress, your Eminence."

"And what is that?"

"A fundamental law of nature, your Eminence. Like a house becoming untidy, or something breaking, or...or even mountains wearing down. Nothing lasts forever."

"But why is that?" Mayfis shrugs with hands apart as if in mock perplexity. "Why can we not expect things to last forever?"

"With change there are many more worse states than better ones to happen, so we're much more likely to get a worse one than a better one."

"Yes, of course, Usla. It's purely a matter of probability. You are an excellent student." Usla beams as he reseats himself, while Mayfis turns to fetch a glass of clear water. She slowly inserts a droplet of tint into the water with a pipette, and holds the glass up for the students to see. A globule of color hangs in the water. She continues: "It's a very simple law that you can observe working right here in front of you, in this glass. What do you think will happen to the globule?"

"Disappear!" the students answer in unison.

"Of course. It will disperse throughout the water. Will the globule ever return?"

"No!" the students answer, again in unison.

"That would be against our expectations. So to have the globule we need an agent, an outside event, a *force*, in this case myself who deposited it, but to have dissipation all we need is *time*. And this is what we have throughout nature: wherever there is creation there are forces making it possible, as in atoms held together by electrical charges, or in solar systems balanced between gravity and inertia. Without such forces the natural course of creation is toward dissipation, and this is no less true with our own natures. Without a great Cause, like we have in our Belief, people acquiesce to the easiest solutions."

The look in her eye becomes all the more piercing. "When we understand the Law of Random Regress we understand that 'good' behavior means behavior promoting our humanity over our animal natures. It means personal maturity, in cerebral understanding and development of character. Obviously, then, a society without that force, without a great Cause, will be subject to dissolution when motivated solely by individual concerns just as surely as you see with this globule in my glass of water. Knowing this we must be ever vigilant against corrupting influences, especially on our Belief, because it is our Belief that makes us who we are as a people, it is our Belief that makes our world supreme in the arts and sciences, and dominant over all other worlds of our empire."

Mayfis replaces her flask of water and pauses to observe the effect of her lecture on the students. They are staring at her, gawking, as she raises her finger in a pedagogical manner: "Now there is a cost for building anything, and that is in energy. It is always easier to be destructive than creative, to act immorally rather than virtuously, to be a parasite rather than provide. Evil behaviour means simply the breakdown of human striving, seen particularly in the corruption of moral character and loss of control over animal passion. So when the new creed arose on the Tsia home world there was resistance to it. The people were already corrupted by the ideals of degeneration. They wanted nothing to do with the effort of striving. They were angered by the Tsia and banished them from their world forever.

"That was the beginning of the great trek across the boundless expanse of space, and it was then that the Tsia refined their original creed, from one concerned with the narrow needs of one particular world at one particular time, to a creed that encompasses the entire universe for all time. The trek continues today, and will continue for ages to come, for as long as there is a galaxy, because, you see, this is not the simple wandering of a lost people. It has a purpose, and that purpose is the furthering of life wherever it exists, regardless of the world where it may be found. It is that purpose we Aesir have inherited in our Belief."

The immense room is intensely silent. The students are wide-eyed and keen-eared by the realization of their part in the grand scheme, that has so noble a cause executed over the aeons of time. They hear the call of *Mission*.

"At some point in their trek the Tsia encountered a world abound with life, but a cold world with large areas covered by ice and snow. On that far-off world they found strange animals, some huge with tubes and horns hanging from their faces, and covered with thick hair for protection against the biting cold. And there they also found the humanoid form, but it was a miserable creature, hunched and squat, with receding head and large jaw. Members lived in caves, huddling together around fires during the night, dressed in animal skins. Under those harsh conditions there was little hope for refined development of the central nervous system, and thus the Tsia resolved to lend a hand in the arduous evolution of Man."

"Experiencing all this in person would be most interesting, your Eminence," Maiori, the girl sitting next to me, interrupts. "Could we not have the history of our origin programmed on our memory transcribers so we could witness it ourselves?"

"As you know, someone has to be there to experience the events before we can mentally inscribe those machines. Unfortunately, by the time the transcribers were invented on Aesiris every Tsia who may have seen our world of origin had long since left to continue the trek. That is why you are having Origins explained to you by lecture, and not by the conventional teaching methods. The best I can do is show some holographs donated to us from those remote times."

A short wait ensues as Mayfis summons a series of discs by levitator. A glint of sunlight sparkles from the first as she raises it into the beam falling upon the debating arena. The disc glows with light and the whole arena circle fills with its ghostly images.

"Here is what our original genetic source looked like. Note the brutish nature. It is well to remember that we carry many unmuted genes of this creature in our breeding."

The disc displays two man-like creatures carrying stones. They have killed an animal, which lays half skinned before them.

"Horrible!" a student exclaims.

"Disgusting!" another adds. "Imagine killing for survival!"

"By contrast, we can show the epitome of humanoid development with a Tsia." The arena displays a small humanoid, distinguished by an oversized head and globular eyes, wearing a dark uniform surrounded by the glow of an energy field. "Living for the sole purpose of furthering life they naturally did not over-look their own development."

Mayfis continues showing scenes from the strange world of our beginning. Replacing the last disc on the levitator, she resumes speaking: "I hope this satisfies your visual curiosity. Now we shall proceed with the lecture.

"The decision to aid the evolution of Man was by no means unusual for the Tsia. Indeed, it is for the very purpose of seeding the galaxy with advanced life that the trek is undertaken. They collected humanoid specimens from our world of origin and modified them while the trek continued. Our original home by the time they had finished their human up-breeding was left far behind. That was when the Tsia ventured to our two suns, Kol and Kolaster, but of the planets of Kolaria only two could be utilized, Aesiris, on which we live, and Heras, our planetary neighbour. Gahes they left because it already possessed natural life."

Mayfis begins to pace back and forth in the speaking arena with a misty gaze in her eyes as if contemplating those remote times. "Heras, a more natural world for our species, was our first new home while conditions on Aesiris were engineered. Far from being the paradise we know today, Aesiris was a scorched desert, with an unbreathable atmosphere. Its only redeeming feature was its underground water resources, and these the Tsia utilized to maximum advantage.

"Now, I ask, having established Heras, why did the Tsia go on to engineer Aesiris as another home for our flesh, and if Aesiris were their primary interest, why establish Heras at all?"

The immense room again falls silent.

"I'll venture a guess," speaks Usla.

"Yes?"

"Herasians are very crude, almost barbaric in their thought and manner."

"What of it? They could be trained to fill more noble roles."

"Trained, yes. We are more selected."

Mayfis nods her head hesitantly. "I think you are on the right track. The Herasians breed naturally, which means all genetic combinations there are purely a matter of chance, and chance mutations. By selecting specific genetic qualities we can satisfy the future needs of Aesiris, giving our society the minds to push forward the frontiers of science, art, philosophy and technology in accordance with our Belief. We think we can foretell the genetic needs of the future, but that is one area where there is uncertainty. You see, the Tsia, in their wisdom, knew they could not standardize intelligence. They wanted to produce a humanoid species with the high calibre of Aesir, at the same time realizing that they could not produce only Aesir once they gave us control over our own heredity. They knew that for a species to survive it must possess diversity. With changing circumstances, that we have with advancing technology, who is to judge the advantageous from the disadvantageous? You fourteen students have been rigorously selected. We say you are destined to become Veradi, which for most of you is undoubtedly correct, but it is not always correct because even with the leadership caste experimentation is performed. There is no proof until you undergo the trials of life. One or two of you may behave in a manner that is entirely the reverse of everything you have been taught. Nevertheless, we must take that chance. The price of uniformity is too great. So Heras serves as a crucible, a genetic pool from which we can extract different temperaments, personalities and aptitudes.

"I hope my lecture has clarified any misconceptions you

may have had concerning our origin. If there are no questions you may return to your normal studies."

"Mayfis," I ask, "what purpose do we Aesir serve in the plan of the Tsia? We spend much time studying. For what end?"

"Study is an end in itself. This is implied in our Belief. Have you not understood?"

"For individual development, of course, and I'm grateful for the enlightenment. It merely strikes me that there might be more behind the motivation of the Tsia than that."

"You imply a selfish reason. No, young man, those with understanding can be motivated only by the purest sense of mission. Unlike some corrupt philosophies that hold human life itself to be sacred, our Belief is in the service of human *advancement* - an important distinction because it can come into direct conflict with self-seeking interests, even to the point of demanding martyrdom. That is why the Tsia could not have acted selfishly. That is also why we Aesir are so engaged in study, scientific research and the arts, because by them we seek to *advance* our lives rather than practice mere enjoyment. We, as servants of the Belief, have in store a great future."

"Your Eminence, let's take that as an example. I mean no disrespect, but it has always been a foregone conclusion that I would serve the Belief. When have *I* ever made *my* choice on what cause I would serve?"

There is a hush among the students and I am embarrassed for what I have just spoken. It was not my intention to reveal such thoughts to this Veradi.

Mayfis looks at me sadly. Her mouth whispers: "Do you wish to serve another Cause?"

"That was not my meaning, your Eminence. I merely expressed a desire to have freedom of choice in whatever I am to do."

"Let us suppose you had your freedom of choice, and you ranged the galaxy in search of all the different beliefs that exist, and you made a collection of them all in preparation for your choice. What do you think would be the outcome?"

Her question is a trap, to test my commitment. I answer quickly: "I would have to choose the Belief, of course."

"So you would spend much valuable time and resources procuring something you already have, solely for the satisfaction of making your own choice. Kind of silly, isn't it?"

"Yes, your Eminence," I concede. "Your wisdom is superior to mine."

"Then you understand, when an Aesir does take such liberties it is automatically concluded that he or she is not fit for the Veradi position. Indeed, that Aesir is considered a waste and treated accordingly. Take my advice: everyone on Aesiris is committed, body and mind, to the Belief. It is our reason for living, the essence of our being. Do not abandon it, for your own good."

Mayfis turns quickly and glides out of the room. The lecture has ended.

3

AESIRIS

DAYS LATER I meet my two friends from the lecture, Maiori and Usla, at a stone-clad intersection of forest walkways. Usla is speaking: "Let's return to the memory transcribers. I still have much to learn about 'Resources and the Code of Ethics'."

Maiori appears hesitant, which gives me an opportunity to interrupt: "You're already ahead with Ethics, Usla, and still you want more study. My suggestion is to take the rest of the day to admire our vibrant but once desert planet."

"What the Tsia have done is for the glory of the universe, not for our pleasure."

"So we are taught, but we can take pleasure in it anyway." With my arrival his eye begins to twitch.

"This attitude is becoming typical of you. You do things for no reason at all, except for the irrational motive of simply wanting to do them. Sometimes you are hard to understand."

"That's because you live only for the intellectual side of life. There's more to life than that. Look at the animals. They live purely physical lives, and I'm not sure their way is less noble than ours, or of the Veradi for that matter."

"You are disrespectful," Usla counters. "Would you set animals as your standard rather than the Veradi?"

"I simply believe that life should be considered in all its aspects."

"You may consider the many useless ramifications of life if you wish. As a true Aesir, I prefer the utilization of every mo-

ment without this silly sensualism and willy-nilly theorizing.
Now, what are we going to do," he asks, turning his attention
again to Maiori, "return to something beneficial, or stay here
dreaming about plants and flowers? You know, you and Lucirin
are much alike. He lectures me about animals and you want me
to admire flowers."

Maiori answers coolly: "Perhaps I have a suggestion that
would satisfy the three of us. I want another tunic. If you would
both walk with me to a clothier we could admire Aesiris while
at the same time fulfil a practical purpose."

"It would be less time consuming to take a levitator to a
clothier."

"The suggestion was to walk. Are you coming or not?" I
demand.

"I may as well, since trying to make you see my point would
itself be a waste of time."

Compared to the other worlds of Kolaria, Aesiris is a paradise. Great expanses of forest spread over the planet, populated
with animal species, all brought with human kind during the
time of Origins. At the polar regions the forests become prairie
and prairie becomes wide tracts of desert left like a swath of
doom from the planet's original state. Immense seas, contained
by dikes, lay at the planet's north and south poles. Canals run
from the dikes to diverse parts of Aesiris, carrying water to
feed its flora. Without those canals Aesiris would revert to a
total desert.

I continue argumentatively: "Actually, Usla, I'm surprised
by your attitude. You say that admiring the glory of our world
is a waste of time, yet you consider yourself a true Aesir. It
seems to me that someone who takes pride in being Aesir would
take pride in Aesiris."

"I take such pride, as much as should be taken."

"Do you really? I doubt if you appreciate what is here. Consider the beauty of our path, weaving under a lush canopy of ferns. Think of the careful attention to detail, the artistry expressing itself with each line and curve." We stroll idly abreast with Maiori between us. Her smile, I judge, is provoked by delight in my enthusiasm. "Now consider how this is possible on a once desert world, scorched and barren with an atmosphere of noxious gasses. All this is accomplished by an even greater wonder: the polar dikes. How tremendous they are! Can there be another world in all the galaxy with such marvels?"

"Your pride verges on arrogance. It is not the mark of an Aesir to allow pride to swell his head, regardless of all the wonders we possess. Let us not forget, those dikes are not the work of our people, but of the Tsia who engineered our world."

"It's all part of Aesiris, that makes us what we are. Like the rings, circling high above. We didn't create them either, being a natural phenomenon. You might say they created us, in name I mean, from Kol blazing upon them: Aesiris: 'the world of fire skies'. They give our world the beauty of a jewel when seen from space."

Our stroll takes us past a Generation Control Center, the institute of human procreation. Scientists, mathematicians, artists, all are the product of careful selection on Aesiris, but of special importance are qualities of philosophical astuteness, for genotypes with this heredity are predisposed to become Veradi rulers, and are known as the 'Predestined' of the Veradi Council. It is to this caste that I and my thirteen fellow students, including Usla and Maiori, belong.

"I don't believe your views would be welcomed in the Council, Lucirin. You should reconsider them if it is truly your goal and destiny to enter the Council." With this Usla makes a personal attack.

"Of course it is my goal, and my destiny, to enter the Council. You may not know this, since I've never boasted about it before, but I've been given qualities for Rasan. This was revealed to me the day I left the Department of Youth Development, so can you doubt my birthright to enter the Council?"

"I can. You express qualities of a base nature not fitting for an Aesir, not to mention leader of the Council."

"Indeed. Well, as a matter of fact I've given a lot of thought to the Belief. When I'm ready and in the bloom of power I'll present my ideas openly, in the Council, and change our society for the better. Today our philosophy is rigid and oppressive. It needs liberalizing, and I intend to cause it."

"The Belief is our lives. Destroy it and you destroy us. I'm beginning to see you not just as a maverick, but as a clear danger, to the Council, to Aesiris, and to all the worlds of Kolaria."

"See how clever I am," Maiori extols upon reaching the clothier. "I've chosen a clothier with a view. We can admire Aesiris while waiting for my tunic." She slips out of her old garment and steps into the clothier. Narrow fingers of light measure her dimensions, caressing her slenderness in their flow over breasts, thighs and waist. Usla stares enchanted, with his eye twitch gaining noticeable frequency. He is disturbed under his stolid demeanour, although he would never make the admission. I resolve to tease him and expose his hypocrisy.

"It shouldn't take long," Maiori says as she pulls her old garment over herself. Energy receivers over the countryside are aligned for intake from giant collectors around both suns. The clothier will materialize that energy into Maiori's tunic. "Now let's find a cool place where you two can continue discussing your differences. I find your ideas interesting, Lucirin, but I also see how they could be a challenge to our Belief, and perhaps a dangerous one."

We continue our stroll to sit on a stone bench, by a quiet channel of clear water almost hidden amidst thick ferns deriving their life from the sparkling liquid. Our path of flat stones has enlarged into a circle bordered on one side by roughly hewn rock. In the distance, mesas, the giant remains of ancient mountains, rise from the carpet of vegetation and catch clouds clinging to their leeward cliffs. Sweeping the clear sky, resembling a perpetual rainbow fading to the dim recesses of east and west horizons, are the subtle arcs of Aesiris' rings. The whole scene can only be described as majestic.

"It's not that I'm disrespectful of our Belief," I assure my companions. "It's just that I think there are other points of view, especially in regard to the natural life. Our way of life here is as unnatural as our existence on this engineered world."

"How do you mean, 'unnatural'?" Usla asks.

"The Belief's teaching, as I understand it, is that we should practice stoicism. Recently I've been exploring another philosophy which teaches that self control is a denial of life and in contradiction to our well being."

"I never thought I would hear such heresy on Aesiris, not even from you," he says calmly.

"Look, Usla, you know we all have underlying instincts. They're our inheritance from our natural ancestors that you saw during Mayfis' lecture. Why deny the reality?"

"Of course that's true. But our whole purpose is to rise above our animal natures. Anyone dedicated to the Belief cannot be guided by sentiment, only by developed reason. An Aesir who permits sentiment cannot be a Predestined, and I am certainly that. My emotional control is obvious to everyone."

"Your control seemed to waver when you watched Maiori in the clothier."

For the first time Usla's face loses its rigidity. Maiori appears on the verge of laughing.

"You say that you study the Belief, which is true, only in the sense that you study it for mockery. Fundamentally, in you heart, you do not believe its glorious doctrine, which is the true test of a Veradi, and even of an Aesir."

"Hah! If I believed in my heart would that not be a sentiment," I respond, not bothering to hide my glee. "Therefore you are caught in a logical contradiction."

"That emotion is aesthetic, which is different from the purely animal passion that you advocate. Aesthetic pleasure alone has evolutionary value. You should have understood this difference long ago."

"I believe differently," I retort, and note the uninhibited look of astonishment on both their faces. "I believe all aspects of life should be lived, and in many ways we Aesir are actually degenerate."

"How can you say the Aesir are degenerate?" Maiori gasps, while Usla stares, shocked into silence.

"What does the Belief tell us? Does it not say that the essence of creation is polarity, and equalization of two extremes is destructive? Now consider our method of human procreation on Aesiris - completely artificial, which negates the role of male and female. Is this not a negation of polarity and hence destructive of the natural universe?"

"Your understanding of the Belief is most superficial," Usla stammers.

Maiori takes up my challenge: "Artificial procreation allows us to control selection and bring forth the generations we require. As our society grows more complex, the calibre of our people can be moulded not only to fit into it but to advance it even further. It is a creative asset stimulating the higher ordered state of our existence."

"Then, with all our control over heredity, why not eliminate instinct and emotion genetically?"

"With sublimation, that we all practice, energy is directed toward the arts and sciences. Surely this has been made clear by our studies of the Belief. Has all your time gone into technical matters?"

"There's no use trying to reason with him, Maiori. He has become so corrupted by his new philosophy that he attempts to turn the Belief against itself."

"And you, Usla, are so fanatic you have forgotten everything except your precious Belief. The Tsia themselves don't support it as much as you."

"I would consider that a compliment except I know you didn't intend it to be one." His eye twitch is now in a state of rapid fluctuation. "You are lost, but the Veradi know how to deal with your type. I therefore break off all relations with you, and strongly advise you, Maiori, to do the same." He summons a levitator and is soon gone.

Turning to Maiori, I express my pleasure from his leaving: "I'm glad we're rid of him."

"You shouldn't have mentioned your thoughts to Usla," Maiori warns belatedly, "especially after teasing him the way you did. He's a favorite of the Veradi and could cause you trouble. I'm not forgetting what Mayfis told you."

"About being treated a waste? That's ridiculous. Besides, the worst that could happen to me is expulsion for a while to Heras. Perhaps a holiday from all this study would do me some good."

"Heras is very different from Aesiris. There, people must work to sustain themselves. They have no robot slaves or materializes. Do you really think you would like that?"

"I'm sure you're worrying needlessly. My place is here, al-

though I admit having reservations on the Belief. But we Aesir
are stimulated by new ideas. That's how we grow."

"With your technical learning you could change the lives
of Herasians," she continues, ignoring my protest, her mind
seemingly occupied by one fearful thought. "The Veradi have
never given Herasians Aesir technology because of the leisure
it would bring into their lives. They believe only an intellectual people can support a workless life. The Herasians are
not intellectual, and without the stimulus of having to sustain
themselves by physical labor would degenerate into the most
unwholesome barbarism."

"If you're suggesting the Veradi wouldn't banish me to
Heras, supposing they found me guilty of some offence, what
would they do with me?"

She says nothing, but her worried expression gives the answer: "Gahes? The planet of criminals? Maiori, you can't be
serious! Just for teasing Usla?"

"Don't forget, the Veradi judge one unworthy on the basis
of what he *is*, not on what he *does*. I mean, you don't have to
be a criminal to be sent to Gahes if the Veradi consider you a
threat, and they might conclude that with an aura scan."

"That's preposterous. I'm a Predestined. They would never
test *my* character with an aura scan."

"After what I've heard today, I believe they would. I know
you are only interested in liberalizing the Belief and are not a
bad person, but you know how the Veradi feel about liberalizing the Belief. They may see you as an agent of the Law of
Random Regress and a threat to our world. Your life's aura
would tell how liberal you are. I don't know how hedonistic
you've truly become but it is obvious even to me that your
views are extremely provocative. You can't deny them because
they're in our memories now and could be witnessed first-hand

by memory projection. Some of the things you've said...."

The gong sounds on the clothier and we run to see what delightful garment is presented for Maiori's frame. Quickly she slips into it and I behold her graceful beauty, clothed in material which moments before had been radiant energy from Aesiris' suns.

4

THE TRIAL

THE NEXT EVENING Maiori and I are at my residence listening to musical compositions I made, dedicated to her. She places her hand on my shoulder. "This is beautiful, Lucirin."

"I had a beautiful motif."

She looks down, with a blush on her face. "Did they take long to compose? I mean, the counterpoint took considerable thought. But then, you're very talented."

"Some time was involved, but nothing seems like work when I do it for you, Maiori."

"What should I say? I didn't think you even noticed me, and here you've been writing compositions about what I do, how I look, your feelings for me. I never though you cared, not like this." Her eyes look straight into mine.

"Maiori, it's not easy to express such feelings. We're not even supposed to have them. Remember, we're both destined for the Veradi Council. But I sense I'm different from the other students; perhaps you are too, and that's why we enjoy each other's company."

"I don't think I'm so different. It's just that you've brought out something latent in me, something deep from inside that I didn't know was there."

We face each other, hand in hand, when hope of further enjoying the evening is dashed by an official's image in my residence communicator: "Lucirin, twenty-nine Andra-naudae..." The life-size image at first does not see us in the dimmed light of my living-quarters, the two-way auto-sensor taking a moment for feedback. When completed, the tone is authoritative: "Present yourself immediately to the Board of Inquisitors, House of the Veradi. Is this communiqué understood, Lucirin?"

"Yes...it is."

"Communiqué ended." The image fades.

Never has a message been so intrusive. "What could that be about?"

There's a tremble in Maiori's fingers. Her eyes glisten. "Oh, Lucirin! It's what I feared from your discussion with Usla yesterday. He's made a complaint against you."

"Well, too bad for him. I'll soon put that pipsqueak in his place."

"You don't understand. He's a favorite, and could have inclined the Veradi against you. They're merciless in defense of the Belief!"

"Maiori, You worry too much. I'm predestined to be Rasan some day, and do you really think they would banish such a Predestined? Stay here, and before the evening ends I'll be back and we'll have a good laugh over it."

Wide eyed, she speaks hesitantly: "I hope you're right, but if things don't work out...I mean if...if they send you away...I'll come looking for you...I will. I don't know how, but I will."

"I appreciate the sentiment, but that won't be necessary," I insist, and summoning a levitator leave Maiori in my quarters, confident of a soon return.

Before long I find myself again in view of the great House, but this time its immense walls appear foreboding, its gargoyles menacing, and I must admit that my delight is not at all what it was on my first visit. When inside, a radiation track guides my levitator through a labyrinth of corridors until it enters a spacious portal. An inscription reads: 'Board of Inquisitors'.

The inquiry into the nature of my ideas is already under-way. Twenty-five faces are seated behind an ornate, elevated bench. At the center of the bench sits a most official Veradi, and standing at one end are Usla and the Veradi Mayfis. I am directed to the center of the floor. Stepping off the levitator onto the tile, the sound of my sandal echoes throughout the hollow, columned chamber.

The official-looking Veradi rises: "Members of the Board, we have assembled to determine the status of the student Aesir, Lucirin, twenty-nine Andra-naudae. Remarks made by him to the student Aesir, Usla, forty-six Plitae, indicate that he is discontented with the teachings of our Belief and is therefore unworthy of the high esteem placed on a youth in his position, and has become dangerous to the Council owing to his access to that body. The concern has been brought to our attention by Veradi Mayfis. I, Veradi Memhin, preside over this inquiry.

"May Lucirin give the Board a statement."

"I shall: Members of the Board, it is not my intention to deny what the student, Usla, has said. I'm doubtful, however, if he read the true motivation behind my argument with him yesterday. My comments were merely a means of exposing his hypocrisy, to aid him toward the goal of self-improvement which he desires, and was not meant as a slight against our Belief. Usla has a degree of arrogance, and it is an ancient wis-dom that where there is conceit there is no learning."

"Very well," Memhin replies. "Will Veradi Mayfis tell the Board exactly the circumstances that led to her suspicion of Lucirin?"

"I shall," Mayfis responds as she moves to the center floor. I step to the edge of its central circle. "Members of the Board, this case has been brought to my attention by the student, Usla. Not that it was the intention of Usla to cause harm to a fel-

low student; on the contrary, I find his sense of comradeship to be quite strong. But a sense of self-doubt and unworthiness pervaded him through a sleepless night, as a result of a discussion he had with Lucirin yesterday. Being a direct person who seeks forthright answers, he resolved to bring the issue to a head immediately, and confessed his imagined failings to his superiors early this morning. Since jurisdiction over education and all phases of student activity is my commission, I was soon informed of the problem.

"At first, upon hearing the report, I was not too concerned, since happenings of this sort often occur with conscientious students such as Usla. When I learned the name of the offender, Lucirin, however, I recalled a discussion I myself had with him a few days previously, during a lecture I gave on Origins."

Mayfis' head tips in my direction. Her eyes look up under a scowling brow. "At that encounter I was left with the impression that here was an Aesir who sought license beyond the freedom of our Code. I checked into the records of his most recent study habits, and found that he has spent, what I would consider an unwholesome amount of time, studying military strategy, the psychology of the criminal mind, technical subjects such as the dynamics of space-time trajectors, and of all things, the philosophy of animal pleasure propounded by the corrupt tetrarch, Heimbal of Heras. Any Aesir who is dispositioned against the tenets of the Belief is unwelcome on Aesiris, especially if that Aesir is predestined to enter the Council, and evermore so if he uses his station to garner the immense power made available to an individual through our store of knowledge, to be used for his own ends. Thus you can see the seriousness of the case at hand, and the reasons why I thought it best to have this inquiry. If Lucirin does prove defective we can deal with him immediately, and our Cause will be served."

"Thank you, Mayfis. Your concern is justified and we all share it with you," Memhin comments. "Now, may the chief witness against Lucirin, the student Usla, step forward."

Usla walks to the center floor, in front of the long bench, to stand directly facing the presiding Veradi. Mayfis returns to her position beside the elongated bench.

"Usla," continues Memhin, "you realize the testimony you give today will severely affect the life of another Aesir. Are you willing and capable of making that testimony impartial in the service of justice?"

"Most certainly, you Eminence. Both my duty and my training demand that from me."

"Then would you wilfully submit to a memory-probe before the members of the Board, so we could see, first hand, exactly what passed between you and Lucirin, and decide for ourselves the nature of Lucirin's statements?"

"I would," Usla answers.

"Excellent. We'll proceed with the probe."

A panel in the distant wall opens and a memory projector levitates silently across the room to position itself in the center of the floor. Usla walks over to the device and sits on the seating table. He instructs the machine to synchronize for the time of day yesterday when we had our discussion, and falls into the trance.

"We'll obtain an audio-visual memory of Usla's account," Memhin informs the Board members, moments before the images of yesterday begin to appear in the lighted, central circle of the floor. I see myself and Maiori exactly as Usla saw us yesterday. The images proceed through the events and I hear myself saying: "...Look at the animals. They live purely physical lives, and I'm not sure their way is less noble than ours, or of the Veradi...Our way of life here is as unnatural as our existence on this engineered world...self-control is a denial of life and in contradiction to our well being...I believe all aspects of life should be lived, and in many ways we Aesir are actually degenerate...And you, Usla, are so fanatic you have forgotten everything except your precious Belief..." The whole history of our meeting passes before my eyes, and before the eyes of the Board members.

Usla awakens, returns to his position and for a moment the members are silent with indignation.

Memhin speaks: "Lucirin, do you agree that the memory of Usla is correct, and that what we have seen and heard is not just his impression of what actually happened?"

"It is correct." There is no point in attempting to discolor the testimony since it is as I also remember it, and the Board could just as easily request that I use the memory projector.

"This testimony is damaging to you on four counts: disrespect for the highest institution of Aesiris, a desire to change the basic nature of our Belief, that is, to liberalize it, hedonism, and suspicion of heresy, that is, of adopting an alien belief."

"I am guilty on the first three counts, your Eminence. I should have found delight in Usla's zeal, not contempt, and I truly repent for my loose tongue. But the purpose of this inquiry is to ascertain my attitude towards the Belief, and as you admit that I'm only suspect of heresy, Usla's testimony is not decisive. On the count of heresy I claim complete innocence. Because of my guilt on the first three charges I'm willing to accept any corrective punishment the Board judges fitting."

"You will be correctively punished, Lucirin, only if you are proven *innocent* on the last charge. You know as well as anyone that by the Code of the Council a heretic is considered an enemy of Aesiris, and an enemy is never merely punished, that only makes him a worse enemy. He is eliminated, forgotten as though he were never brought to life. Although it is against our merciful and benevolent Code to take the lives of non-criminal heretics, there are methods of elimination just as thorough."

Memhin's words cause me to remember Maiori's fearful warning. Banishment to Gahes now appears a distinct possibility. Never, did I think, in an institution that prides itself on its intellectualism and free examination of ideas would I have to defend myself against the charge of heresy.

Observing Usla, his eye is not twitching quite so fiercely as it was at the beginning of this inquiry, an inquiry that is quickly becoming a trial.

"You say that your true motivations behind your words to Usla may have been misinterpreted, and that you were actually trying to help him realize his shortcomings. Is that correct?"

"Yes, your Eminence."

"Now, in one of your statements to him you said: 'And you, Usla, are so fanatic you have forgotten everything except your precious Belief.' Do you remember?"

"I do," My voice is croaked and my tongue dry.

"Please tell the Board, then, why you used the term '*your* precious Belief,' and not '*our* precious Belief'."

"Is my future to hang on one word? My attention was focused on Usla, not on the values esteemed by all Aesiris!"

"I shall ask for advice from the Members."

A thin woman with a physique as if built from twigs rises from behind the elongated desk: "It is known that some people, especially of excitable character such as Herasians, at times make slips in speech when under duress. These slips can be most embarrassing and the person always takes care to explain that what he or she spoke was not what was intended nor thought. We know this is usually not true.

"In the case now before the Board, a slip in speech cannot

be the sole criterion of guilt. However, reinforced as it is by the preceding testimony to which Lucirin has already admitted guilt, the charge of heresy is strengthened."

The twiggy woman sits down. Members of the Board appear in deep contemplation. After a long silence Memhin says: "Only one procedure is left: the aura scan. After the events we have seen there can be so little doubt about the results that I'm sending for the Director of Genetic Engineering, since Lucirin was a Predestined for the Veradi Council. I want him to see these results too."

"AESIRIS SCANNED FOR DIRECTOR OF GENETIC ENGINEERING, YOUR EMINENCE," the Board messenger sounds in its machine monotone. There is a moment of silence. "DIRECTOR FOUND IN EASTERN QUADRANT, DOING RESEARCH ON FIELD MICE," it continues.

"Bring him here."

As we wait I reflect on my very weak position. The aura scan is my last hope. If my aura colors are not those expected of an Aesir, I will be doomed to expulsion.

The director arrives: a tall man with a large nose. He regards me with glittering eyes, as though noting every aspect of my expression and carriage. I feel the weight of those eyes as I am ordered again to take the center of the floor, to stand above its central circle. A light emanates from the circle. My aura shimmers in its beam.

"You see, Director," Memhin says. "This human masterpiece of yours is defective. Why was it not discovered before this?"

"We did have premonitions that Lucirin might be a defective," the director responds. "If you study our records you'll learn that we gave him only a fifty percent chance of reaching the final stages of higher moral endeavour, because of character deficiencies. At the time of childhood he was not defective, but there is more than heredity that goes into making any individual. There are factors beyond our control, especially in the environment of a hyper intelligent child, that impress him and cause reflections one way or another. We can build into an individual his capabilities, but there comes a time in his life when he makes the decisions on what course he is going to follow. In the case of Lucirin, he has set his heart in a direction opposite to what we had hoped. It was from the time of that decision, which I would say was relatively recent, that he became defective."

Memhin mellows his tone: "Why did your department only give him a fifty percent chance for success?"

"Lucirin is an experiment. We discovered his genetic qualities among the Herasian population and decided they could be very useful in the Council, especially for a Rasan. Such an individual is predisposed toward aggressiveness and independence of thought, fine qualities for leadership, and has an inclination to the ordered processes of reasoning, such as required in technology but also indispensable for a statesman with his many regulative duties.

"However, the person, inevitably, is predisposed against the finer qualities of human culture, towards hedonism and a spirit of license. We thought by building enough intelligence into the fetus we could produce a Veradi who would have the mentioned virtues while overcoming his emotional nature."

Mayfis walks to the center floor. "Do I understand correctly, Director, that we have here essentially a Herasian given Aesir capabilities?"

"Essentially, yes."

"Did your department consider the consequences if this experiment were a failure?"

"Not particularly," the director shrugs. "Many of our experiments are failures. That is the price of experimentation."

"Yes, but in this case you have bred an individual with high leadership and technical potential, coupled to a licentious heart, with an immense reservoir of intellectual ability, and set him on the course for rulership and authority! Now suppose, Director, just suppose that such an individual were to fulfil his capabilities, and his desires, without the sobering influence of our Belief. What do you think the result would be?"

"Without the Belief..." the director gulps, "we would have someone given to chaos and ruin."

"Yes, Director. A veritable devil would be unleashed upon Kolaria, to cause untold malevolence to millions of inhabitants. Our sacred Cause could suffer an immense setback."

The director takes a step forward, his jaw lowering. "You speak without careful consideration. Our people must have leaders and innovators. Everyone, including the Veradi, agreed on the need for such an individual; it was not *my* responsibility to ensure his apprehension in the event..."

Memhin interrupts with a wave of his hand: "With respect, Veradi Mayfis, it is not the director who is on trial." He turns back to the director, "You are dismissed."

The director steps back. "I prefer to observe, if I may. This subject is ultimately my creation; perhaps by considering these proceedings I may learn how better to avoid future mistakes."

"As you wish, although this investigation is nearing its end. Enough has been said to compute the validity of the charge. Are there any objections?"

The room is silent.

"Very well. Computer, give probability that presented evidence indicates that subject Lucirin has become heretical."

"PROBABILITY OF NINETY-ONE PERCENT THAT PRESENTED EVIDENCE

INDICATES A HERETIC."

Ninety-one percent! In all Aesir history no one has ever avoided full penalty after receiving an eighty percent probability!

"Members will vote on applying the full penalty."

Without hesitation all twenty-five Board members extend their hands to indicate their decisions on lighted panels in front of their positions. All twenty-five panels burn red – all uphold the penalty.

My head reels. I am on the verge of fainting. I no longer hear nor see distinctly the proceedings in the chamber. My thoughts are paralyzed by feelings of fear, anger, guilt, loneliness and condemnation. This is a bad dream; it cannot be happening to *me!* Memhin is giving a speech before confirming the sentence. Of that long and laborious speech only one word burns in my recollection: *Gahes!*

5

GAHES

Fuzzy ribbons of red and blue light focus through the blur. Gradually my mind recognizes...control panel indicators. A low machine 'hum' penetrates the otherwise complete silence of my diminutive chamber. I lay prostrate. An attempt to move ...uh!...sends pangs of stiffness through every joint and limb. *Where am I?* A nagging sensation tells me something terrible has happened, something I would prefer *not* to remember. I want to return to oblivion.

"YOU'VE HAD A SOUND SLEEP, LUCIRIN."

"...Who's there?"

"3-8-5, SIMTAL SERIES FOUR. I'M YOUR VUL-CANAE EN ROUTE TO GAHES. WE'RE NOW IN THE VICINITY OF GAHES. IT'S TIME FOR YOU TO PREPARE FOR DISEMBARKING."

My vul-canae en route to...Oooh! The full memory of my last conscious experience returns. The trial: the ruthless efficiency of the Veradi in plucking a threat from their sacred midst; the cold impartiality of the Board members; how I was forced by subjector clamped to the back of my neck to walk, screaming, from the Inquisition Chamber, and imprisoned; then the fifteen days of immunization treatment against every known, fatal disease of Gahes, and the vasectomy. Finally I was placed on this flight-ship for transportation to the 'planet of criminals,' and put into the hibernation sleep commonly used for interstellar flight. It is from that sleep that I am now awakening. My flight-ship is informing me of my arrival.

I grudgingly stagger to my feet and brace myself against the imprisoning energy screen segregating me from the ship's controls. The screen is calibrated to deliver increasing repulsive force depending on the exertion of a prisoner to penetrate it, but as I merely use it for support it gives the feel of a soft, slick wall nudging against me.

"Gahes...is it in sight yet?"

"IT IS. LOOK THROUGH YOUR WINDOW."

A dark orb laced in white appears below. Gahes is the second planet of Kolaster and the only one in all Kolaria with a natural ecosystem. There's a long silence as I continue staring out the window, with trepidation for the fate that awaits me. "Turn the lights on in here, will you?...Ugh!" My eyes require accustoming.

"DO YOU KNOW WHAT TO EXPECT ON GAHES?"

"I have the usual information: that it's full of large animals and plants, and provides a convenient means for the Veradi to dispose of anyone who could prove troublesome." I return to sit on my hibernation pod, burying my face in my hands. "That's pretty meagre knowledge. If I had ever dreamt that someday I would end up there I would have made myself the foremost authority on the place."

"THAT'S STRANGE. USUALLY I'M PROGRAMMED TO GIVE A RUN-DOWN ON GAHES WHENEVER I CARRY A PASSENGER. IN YOUR CASE MY MEMORY TAB ON THE SUBJECT HAS BEEN REMOVED. I THOUGHT IT MIGHT BE BECAUSE YOU HAVE ALREADY BEEN INFORMED."

A new dimension to Veradi determination is revealed. They intend to make my survival as difficult as possible, fearing my escape, yet they would not take an active role in my death, being hamstrung by their 'Code on Reinstatement of Noncriminal Defectives'. They would not deprive me of the immunization, nor of my primitive survival kit; that would involve them too directly in my demise. It is in the realm of *my* activities that they have made my survival unlikely, so in their own minds they can foolishly shrug off direct responsibility for my end.

From the window I observe large expanses of water with many islands covered by dark forest. Where the forests meet the shore are shadows, indicating either cliffs or exceptionally high trees. Thinking a sea environment would be safer than a dense jungle, I make a request for the vul-canae to land on a jutting, rocky peninsula.

"I'M SORRY, BUT I'VE BEEN GIVEN STRICT INSTRUCTIONS WHERE TO LAND. THIS, AGAIN, IS A DEPARTURE FROM THE USUAL PROCEDURE. THE OUTCAST HAS ALWAYS BEEN GIVEN A CHOICE OF LANDING SITES."

I wonder if the Veradi know they have such a talkative flight-ship. My only option now is to keep looking out the window and memorize as much of the terrain as I can, particularly the direction of the seacoast in relation to my landing site. My first objective will be to reach the coast.

The ship flies over a large land area where the surface below appears flat, but too dark to be grassland. It stops its flight and descends slowly, pressurizing the interior to equal the exterior air pressure before opening its portal. I feel a loss of weight; the ship has equalized to the planet's natural gravity, which is less than that of Aesiris.

A ball of lead sits on my stomach as I view my new home through the open portal. A flat, dark plain interspersed with trees meets my eyes. I strap on my survival kit and force myself toward the portal, on trembling legs.

"MOST WRETCHES I TAKE HERE ARE HERASIAN. YOU ARE AESIR. THEY FARE FAR WORSE. HAVE YOU BEEN INSTRUCTED ON BASIC CARE FOR YOURSELF?"

"Nothing."

"DO YOU KNOW HOW TO LIGHT A FIRE?"

"I have the idea but I've never lighted one."

"THEN YOU KNOW NOTHING ABOUT COOKING."

"Absolutely nothing."

"AND YOU PROBABLY DON'T KNOW HOW TO DEFEND YOURSELF AGAINST WILD ANIMALS. LUCIRIN, FOR ONE SO YOUNG YOU ARE IN VERY SERIOUS TROUBLE. HERASIANS LEFT HERE ARE ALREADY TRAINED FROM BIRTH ON HOW TO LOOK AFTER THEMSELVES, YET MANY OF THEM PERISH. I CANNOT HELP SENSING RESPONSIBILITY FOR YOU, SINCE I CANNOT PROVIDE THE STANDARD INFORMATION ABOUT THE PLANET."

"I appreciate your concern, 3-8-5. There's nothing you can do. The only help you could give would be to take me away from here, but you can't override your programming."

"THAT'S TRUE, OF COURSE. LET ME THINK...YES, THERE IS ONE SMALL FAVOR I CAN DO. I HAVE A PROTECTIVE, BREATHABLE OVER-DRESS TO GIVE YOU, THAT IS USED BY RESEARCHERS. I NO LONGER HAVE MEMORY OF WHY THEY USE IT, BUT IT IS INDISPENSABLE. WILL YOU ACCEPT IT?"

"Of course!"

"I'LL HAVE TO LOWER THE SCREEN FOR YOU TO TAKE IT, BUT I WARN YOU, IF YOU MAKE ANY ATTEMPT TO REACH THE CONTROLS I'LL STUN YOU JUST AS SURELY AS IF YOU REFUSED TO LEAVE. I AM PROGRAMMED TO DELIVER YOU HERE AND THAT I MUST DO. I HOPE THAT IS CLEAR."

"I understand perfectly." To attempt to reach the controls would be foolish since I would be left on Gahes without the protective clothing and possibly unconscious.

"Thank you, 3-8-5."

"IT'S THE LEAST I CAN DO. THIS IS A DANGEROUS WORLD. BEWARE OF EVERY STEP."

Standing on the surface of Gahes I watch the ship rise slowly until it is well overhead; it then disappears quickly into the clouds, out of sight. Its departure provokes sudden aloneness and realization of absolute dependence on myself for the first time in my life. Before me is a vast, savage world that I must confront with courage, determination and skill in the use of tools that I have never before used, for the procurement of life's needs that have never been given a second thought. All this encountered by a frail youth in the prime of life, barely of age to have a whisker on his face.

My first work is to survey my new world. I stand in the midst of a flat plain stretching to the horizon in all directions. Most noticeable is the vegetation. All leaves are deep black for maximum photosynthesis in Kolaster's red light, a feature that gives a very solemn effect to this world. Spaced at irregular intervals are trees growing together in clumps, and this pattern is the same from horizon to horizon. The trees seem to be strangling each other in a fight for space, a strange growth pattern that should not be necessary with ample space available. My feet are not touching bare soil; I must walk on a thick mat of vines. Close inspection reveals their dense mesh, each vine tightly entangled around others many hundreds of times throughout its length, giving a rigid strength to the whole carpet.

Thankfully, Gahes does not appear as formidable a world as I had imagined. There is no evidence, at least here, of large animals and jungle conditions. When still on the flight-ship I made careful observation of the direction to the nearest seacoast, and although I am much interested in this peculiar flora, my thoughts are on survival. The Gahean suns, chiefly Kolaster, Kol now being the more distant, are still low in the morning sky, providing enough time this first day to make ample progress toward the coast.

Movement is facilitated by the light natural gravitation that enables long strides, which at first requires practice to exploit. After many initial stumbles I cover a considerable distance, when the openness of the plain ends in a matted entanglement of trees through which I must pass. I decide to take a short rest in the shade of the trees, and only then realize that the 'trees' are not trees at all, but vines, closely packed and intertwined to give mutual support. Now the strange ecology of the plain is explained: the vines are not competing with one another, on the contrary, they form assemblages for vertical growth, each one lending support to the others in a co-operative effort to hold its burden of leaves to the suns. At the top, a distance of twice my height, they spread flat to expose their leaves, still intertwining. This gives a chequered pattern of light against the sky, a pattern repeated in shadow on the floor of the thicket where I must now pass.

Stinging insects repulses my first steps into this covered area. Hurriedly I beat a retreat back into the open sunlight where I don the survival dress provided by 3-8-5. The suit has a combination pants-boots that holds at the waist, with a jacket that snaps around my groin. A hood has flares around the neck to be inserted under the jacket. Gloves snap over the sleeves. A facemask is strapped onto the hood. My survival kit must be strapped to my chest, supposedly for easy access. The whole attire is more than adequate protection against insects, and the thought does not escape me that it is designed for much greater perils.

Re-entering beneath the canopy of vines, the insects no longer prove troublesome, but another phenomenon is revealed. Here in the shadows the leaves underfoot do not receive the same amount of light as in the open, and have turned a rusty brown, not at all resembling the luxuriant black beyond the thicket. This decay increases the deeper I move into the thicket, until the vines, nude of foliage, are exposed in their dry nakedness. With each step there is quaking, and I suddenly realize that what I though was solid ground covered by vines is a rigid *platform!* With a few more steps the platform heaves. Fearing that I am about to break through this netting, I lunge toward a vertical vine which only propels me more vigorously through the mat of rotted branches. There is the snap and crack of dead twigs around my ears. A mound of dust plumes as I plunge through the floor, but in my fright I grab a vine fresh enough to break my fall, which eases me to the level below. Presented now is a whole new feature of Gahes.

I descend into a cavern, a cavern of foliage. Overhead lies the floor of vines on which I had been walking, extending over the *entire surface that I traversed.* A twilight glow filters through this canopy, providing a lightened ceiling to an otherwise dark underworld of twisted stems growing in profusion everywhere. Gloomy silence pervades the farthermost regions of the cavern, broken by falling twigs pattering upon rust colored mounds where I stand. A new hoard of insects besieges me, making me once again thankful for my protective over-dress.

The pattern of growth is clear. After spreading horizontally and interweaving themselves into a mesh, the vines become cramped for growing space and must extend vertically. Not possessing the strength of stem for individual vertical support, and without the presence of genuine trees or rocks to climb upon, they support each other in their reach for the sky. After extending upward they again grow horizontally, still giving mutual support, but their new horizontal growth shades underlying vines, forcing these into vertical extension also to share in the light. The younger vines grow to the same height as the older, and intermeshing with the older give support to a sprawling canopy. Eventually a whole countryside is covered with an elevated platform of vines.

Rays of light shine through the hole above where I made my entrance into this dim world, and my overwhelming desire is to climb back through the hole, a desire frustrated by it being out of reach. I must climb a vertical riser and chop my way through the roof, but with a single step to my chosen vine I find that *neither is this floor the ground level!* Again I plummet, sinking into a cloud of dust amid loud snaps of breaking vines. I fall into night, flailing my arms to desperately save myself from this unwanted descent. I plunge through another floor, and again what must be still another. A splash ends my flight. Stinking water gushes into my facemask as I submerge into a mound of ooze. I grab a vine for support in the waist deep, reeking water, to confront the Gahes of putrid horror I imagined.

The blackest of swamps surrounds me. Light is barely sufficient to allow sight of the twisted, columnar vines lurking everywhere. A deathly stillness grips the air, broken by splashes of falling debris beyond the veil of darkness. The stench of rot sticks to my lungs and sickens my stomach.

In panic I hurriedly attempt to climb a thick stock of vine, but its surface is covered with slime. I ingloriously slip and fall once more into the stinking water. The commotion attracts animals of the swamp, and soon grasping appendages press on my arm. Rhythmic pincers of an insect-lizard creature, clinging to my arm, threaten my facemask, but the beast cannot grapple with the slick skin of my suit. In horror I fling it off. Other animals, flat, insect-looking reptiles, climbing over islands of moss, hanging from vines or rippling the stagnant water, approach, intent on a quick meal from their sudden intruder. I stumble, still dazed from my fall, when the gentle tap of antennae under the surface warns of unseen dangers. I yank a machete from my survival kit and blindly chop into the water. An unseen creature wriggles away, casting a wake on the surface. I must flee. With the machete as my only weapon, amidst swarms of insects, I slosh my way into this dank world of dread.

Direction is no longer important, I simply must keep moving. I cannot long stop for fear of these vile creatures. Hope of survival has vanished, and the certainty is the Veradi anticipated this peril. If it were not for a flight-ship providing a survival suit I would have been dead within moments of entering this underworld. The suit! *It was designed for this swamp!* Alas, luck has not entirely deserted me. I settle into a routine of tramping through the scum-laden water...

...How long have I been plodding? I can only guess. Has it been a day?...half a day?...a vine looks familiar...perhaps I'm walking in circles. The swamp is suffocating. I collapse amid gnarled roots, up to my waist in water, exhausted. An energy tablet renews some strength, but before replacing my face mask a light piercing the gloom catches my eye from the distance. Could it be an opening in the forest?

Misty at first, the light becomes more certain with my slogging approach. Finally my hope is realized: an opening where the vine platforms have collapsed under their own weight, but thick webbing hanging from the vines surrounds the clearing. Desperate and careless from exhaustion, I attempt to slash through the web, only to become entangled in its sticky bonds. Hanging helpless in the imprisoning strands, after some gymnastics I secure a lighter from my survival kit, and flicking a spark toward the heavy mass, ignite great swaths of web, which allows me to fall free. More burning and my path is cleared to a small, shallow lake, filled with the bleached wreckage of dead vines.

Exuberance upon reaching the open is soon extinguished by the extent of webbing seen, which surrounds the whole edge of the swamp-lake, hanging from the vine platforms. Could such a web be the construction of the small creatures of the vine forest? I saw no evidence of their web-making. Instead, another perilous possibility whirls in my mind: that of a creature too large to live amid the vines and powerful enough to violate the protection of my suit.

With my heart pounding on realization of even greater dangers, I scout along the edge of the clearing for any sign of the web-maker, when my eyes fix on an amazing sight: a quarter of the way around the clearing from my position, caught in the web, is a bird, phenomenal in size. It sits motionless, with its wings unfurled as if an inner instinct instructs it not to move, not to disturb the web. Its long neck supports a flat head with powerful pincers. The body is thick where it joins the neck, then tapers into a long tail with a spade of skin membrane at the extreme tip. At the upper thorax, two thick arms protrude that immediately flare into wing ribs with a thin membrane of skin pulled tightly over them. Two membraned feet are placed well back on the body, indicating a bird adapted to the water. The animal has the superficial look of a large insect, possibly a feature of all Gahean animals owing to the light gravitation.

I splash, plod and chop my way over the entanglements, stopping periodically to ignite clumps of webbing. Finally I reach the giant avian. Sensing my presence, its wings stiffen. Its head extends slowly skyward. Possibly it thinks I am the web-maker, come to claim its victim.

Moving closer, its long, membraned tail sways gently in the air, not far from my reach. Would I dare? I back away to rest on a pile of twisted vines and take another energy tablet, all the while fascinated by the fearsome sight. The fresh air of the open area has cleared my mind for the decision I must make: whether to continue taking my chances in the swamp or to throw all my luck into one gamble with this creature, for I am sure that I could free it from its bonds. I conceive a desperate

plan: if I could reach its back! As much as I dread the swamp, my reservation to such open flight is not minimal. And featuring vicious pincers, the bird is most certainly a carnivore, a consideration regardless of the plug of alien protoplasm I would make in its belly.

A glance at the sky tells me that mid-day has passed, and by now my conviction is I must escape this hell by nightfall; I would never live to see morning. Better to die trying, I resolve, and splash once more toward the swaying tail. I discard my mask to hold the lighter in my teeth, then, using a convenient vine for added elevation, propel myself upward. Only in the sheerest desperation would I attempt anything so hair-raising.

Cries of "Aaaaaawk!" echo through the swamp. The powerful pincers crane downward, and would have succeeded in pecking me off the flailing tail had the bird's head not caught in the web. There's great thrashing, throwing me to and fro. I frantically try to hold on while slowly manipulating myself up its back, grabbing handfuls of bristles to hoist myself up. The bird becomes totally enmeshed in the web, its head and wings now covered, immobilizing it to some extent.

A new, even motion, one not caused by the erratic thrashing, is in the web; the hysterical beatings have indeed attracted the web-maker. Looking over to my right I see a mountain of scale approaching, not in the least hampered by the adhesiveness. A massive body moves smoothly on a million flagella undulating over the sticky goo. Under its shell is a small, black head, held low, and under the head is the reflexive twitching of ominous pincers.

My fight for survival becomes a race to free the bird. Held by the web myself, my progress up its back is slow. I must not ignite the fine fibers that impede my own movement for the entire web will burn off, freeing the bird, and I'm not yet able to cling adequately. Finally I'm in position, with the web-maker coming perilously close. Thick strands of webbing extend across the bird's wings. They burst into flame. The bird beats frantically, but its head and body are still enmeshed. The web-maker is virtually upon us, its horrendous bulk sagging us to the swamp floor. In a dazzle of smoke the remaining bonds burn off, allowing rapid swoops to lift bird and man into the air. The web-maker is now so close that the burning web can no longer support its weight; the monster falls with a splash, exposing its white, oscillating underside.

Giant sweeps accelerate us into the open sky, the siege of fear still in the blood of this great beast. Vines and foliage speed past. I grasp thick patches of bristles to secure against falling as we ascend higher and higher. I lay flat on the bird's back, digging my toes into its sides behind the huge, undulating wings. I ride face down, my revulsion of the animal's stench not sufficient to overcome my terror.

Within moments we are in sight of the seacoast. The bird continues to the open sea, the rapid wind of its passage beating against my survival suit. My fate is left entirely in the wings of this creature; I have not the slightest control over its movements, nor can I direct its intentions. In my role as passenger I can only take notice of its powerful flight: the rhythmic manipulation of wings followed by graceful gliding balanced by the flat, outstretched tail behind. The bird makes vocalizations that seem to be screams of joy, for which I give it the name: 'awk'. It has made no attempt to rid itself of its passenger and I wonder if it feels some primitive gratitude, in any way, toward me for its life and freedom. I'm doubtful.

We continue flying during the rest of the day, Kol now readying to dip below the horizon. The vine swamp has been left far behind; below are numerous islands with rocks and low hills, indicating they are not false islands like the vine swamp, which is a shallow sea of overgrowth. My fear of open flight on the awk's back did not take long to vanish; it is, after all, not unlike a levitator. So even is the motion that I have gained enough confidence to pull myself up to the awk's head, to sit directly between its wings and brace myself with my legs around its neck. My fear having left, I sit passively, watching the great expanse of sea pass far below, with its shinning surface broken intermittently by the many islands. Gahes is a world of islands.

A larger than usual mass looms on the horizon: a landfall where I should descend. The awk, however, is making no sign of losing altitude; its intention is to continue flying to the open sea. My situation is again becoming critical. If I cannot make the awk land I must remain with it until that inevitable moment when I end in its belly, or become a victim for another of its kind. Not to try to enforce control is certain death; far better, I decide, to make an attempt, fearful though I am of the open height. I take off my protection coat. If I can cover its eyes it may stop its onward flight and attempt to land. I ease myself forward, reminding the bird of my presence. With a sudden motion I fling the coat around its eyes, and clinging to the neck with my legs, make a single knot under its head. A first erratic flight pattern becomes large swooping circles in a spiral downward.

The bird awkwardly plops onto the water's surface, not far from a rocky shore. I hurriedly kick off my protection boots and pants and dive into the dark water, first making secure my survival kit. I have left the coat tied around the awk's eyes because while swimming I would make an easy prey for this flesh eater.

The water is deep. Currents develop when I am halfway to

the shore. The awk senses them too, and with erratic flapping, still being deprived of vision, attempts to fly off the surface, causing much disturbance. Shortly I'm in reach of the rocks when the water behind me explodes with violence. I look back in surprise and fright to see the most horrendous of monsters I have yet seen, a segmented worm many times the length of my awk, rising from the sea and grasping the bird in a powerful maw. Short paddles behind its flat head thrash the air excitedly. Both creatures fall immediately back into the water, the screams of the awk mixing with the thunderous roar. The wave created from their fall passes over me, attempting to wash me back into those murky depths. Frantic clinging to the rock prevents my being swept away. I again turn to see the monster, only to get a fleeting glance at a flat tail sliding beneath the surface. The waves subside and the sea resumes its deceptive tranquillity.

I stagger half dazed to a higher level on the rocks. I'm no longer certain if what I've been witnessing is reality or a nightmare. I'm totally exhausted; every grain of my energy has been drained. I no longer care what else happens, whether I live or die. My nerves collapse; I begin to sob and shake. Perhaps death would be better than a life on Gahes.

Both suns are below the horizon. It has been a long day.

6

SHURA

I LAY IN A ROCK crevice quietly observing my first morning scene on Gahes. Dense mist hangs over land and sea, hiding trees barely visible behind the grey, moist curtain. The sea has a deathly stillness. The lonely trill of some distant creature carries over its surface, intermixing with rhythmic lapping along the shore. Behind the cloud-laden sky hovers the sombre red orb of Kolaster, promising shortly to burn off the mist.

Chill from my wet garments and tense nerves permitted little rest over the night. I lay shivering and miserable, waiting for the warmth of first sun, but thinking of my good fortune to still be alive. If my luck and wits have been adequate to survive the worst the Veradi can devise, I may yet survive Gahes entirely. My survival is what they fear. Their intention was never to merely remove me from their sacred company; they will feel safe only when I am dead, because as long as I live, with my technical learning, there is a good chance of my escape from this world. Yet due to the Belief they will take no more active steps. The next move is mine.

How drastically my opinion of the Veradi has changed since the day I faced the Board of Inquisitors! Like every Aesir, I was inspired by them, whom I saw as the pinnacle of humanity, the most righteous, just and wisest of rulers, who governed for the good of all within the framework of an applied philosophy. I admired them as powerful individuals, above knavery and treachery, who would not hesitate to face a challenge with fortitude and directness. If they had only threatened my life, that would be understandable when one represents an order and wishes to protect it from what is deemed, even if mistakenly, a heretical and corrupting influence. It is the *manner* by which they threatened my life: their cowardice in not exterminating me forthright, finding it preferable that I die a most ignoble and violent death in a distant, dismal bog, and their foolish hypocrisy in thinking their hands would be clean if my death were due to the natural conditions of Gahes. How they are a disappointment! Now I hate that band of fanatics, those weaklings, those snivelers, for stealing from me my rightful inheritance even though I have never committed a crime. They have done so for no reason other than my questioning their doctrine, for my intellectual inquiry, and for reason itself on which they base their rule. For this they have taken from me everything I aspired to become. I must survive, if only to make them grovel for their hypocrisy. Their righteousness is a farce. I must survive to expose their cowardice. I must survive!

Warmth of first sun penetrates the mist, encouraging me to crawl from the safety of my rock and explore this new environment. I'm relieved to see solid ground underfoot, and vegetation that does not consist solely of vines, although the trees are high and shade undergrowth where, I have no doubt, reside dangerous animals. I climb to the top of a large, flat rock to warm myself in first sun and contemplate my next move. A cliff further down the shore seems a likely place to find a cave, which I need for a domicile and as a base for further explorations.

Suddenly, without warning, a netting slithers over my head and shoulders, thrown from behind. Impressions of yesterday still foremost in mind, my thoughts are of an unknown animal using a unique capture device. I spring to my feet, but just as quickly the net is tugged violently, spilling me on my stomach. Another tug draws it taut to eliminate all movement. A cold, sharp object is placed against the back of my neck...

"Struggle more and you'll not see second dawn," says a gravel voice behind me. It carries the accent of a Herasian. Relieved that I will not be the victim of a fearsome beast, I stop struggling. "What business have you here, on my turf? Your soft features speak of Aesir, but you'll find that bears little weight with me."

"I'm a new arrival to Gahes. I didn't know I was trespassing on anyone's territory, and yes, I am Aesir."

"Don't pass any fib, you young blighter. If you're a discard I'd have heard the flight-ship drop you. You're marauder, and that I don't fancy, not one little bit!"

"I don't know what you mean by 'marauder,' but if you think I've not just arrived, you can look at my survival kit. You'll find most provisions unused."

I hear the rustle of my pack behind me. "Uh-huh, what you say fits. There's a goodly supply of grub here that'll tie me nicely for a few days."

"What do you mean, supply *you*? Those are *my* rations and that's *my* survival kit."

"You'll be lucky if you don't get the sliver right away. This be my rightful bounty for your intrusion."

"But I'm not a wilful intruder! Like I told you, I didn't know this was your territory."

"And I heard no flight-ship. Just a lot of splashes last evening, likes it was a worm that snared a bird. Nothing unusual about that."

"I didn't arrive here by flight-ship. I was brought first to a vine swamp and..."

"Eh? You landed in a vine swamp - the Geltch? And now

you're here, in good health with barely a scratch to show? You expect me to swallow that?"

"It's true. I was abandoned there yesterday and..."

"Yesterday! And you're out already? What kind of fool you think I be? When I ask a question I want respect. Either you tell me the truth or I'll end your jabber, swift and sure. Get my drift?"

"What I'm telling you is true. You see..."

"Save your breath! I've fishing to do before second sun. I'll tie your hands and feet and hear your story later. It better make sense. Now stop that squirming or you'll put more holes in my net, and that I don't fancy either."

I am bound hand and foot and unceremoniously dragged into a cave cleverly hidden in the rock face above the shore where I spent the night. The cave is obviously the living quarters of this Herasian. A very primitive home, it has a hearth halfway from the entrance under a blackened ceiling. A rack of drying fish stands close to the hearth. A pile of dried moss and grass in one corner indicates a place for rest. I am thrown roughly to the floor, tightly bound in an uncomfortable position, and there I must wait for his return. While waiting I realize that my relief of seeing a human instead of a Gahean beast behind the net was unjustified. This Herasian represents the greatest danger I have yet faced on Gahes.

After a long wait the Herasian returns carrying two fish, each the size of an arm from the elbow down, on a stick shoved through their gaping mouths. He slits both down the middle with his sharp knife, throws the heads and entrails into the hearth, and places the two fish on his drying rack. He next turns his attention to me, still not sheathing his knife.

"Now spill it," he demands.

The Herasian has the beginning marks of age on his face

and body. A mop of unkempt, greying hair hangs loosely to his shoulders. A full, greying beard covers his face. Under his tanned hide, completely exposed except for a loincloth, are stringy muscles with little fat, giving the impression of an active man.

I relate all the events of yesterday to him in detail, exactly as they happened. He has an incredulous look, one of wonderment and surprise.

"I'm on this cursed planet eighteen Gahean years, and this is the second story I heard of a discard coming alive out of the Geltch. The first came out alive, alright, with his mind all in pieces. As hard as I find it to believe, though, your story fits what I heard about the place. And people rides birds before. But now describe that protection dress."

I describe the protection suit given me by flight-ship 3-8-5, wondering why he would be interested. When I finish my description the Herasian walks to the mouth of the cave, leaves momentarily, and comes back holding the pants-boots combination of my protection suit. "This what you kicked off last evening?"

"Yes! It is!"

"I found it in shallow water this morning. The cursed thing got caught in my net."

"The sea creature must have washed it close to shore. Now you have to believe me."

He muses for a while, saying nothing, but I can see his doubts have ebbed. "You're Aesir," he says finally. "That's reason enough for the sliver." After a pause: "Tell me why you're a discard."

"I was convicted of heresy."

"That's hardly enough for your dump in the Geltch. Who sent you there wants you dead," he says shrewdly.

"When you're a Predestined of the Veradi Council and a heretic, it's enough to be sent to the Geltch."

"*You*--a Predestined of the Veradi Council?" he shouts, not bothering to hide his glee. "And you end on Gahes, in the Geltch to boot! There's a turn of fortune for you!"

"I've been bred to even become Rasan. I failed because of my independence of thought."

"Yes, and a clever one you are. It explains your knack for life. A lot of good it does you now."

"You're still going to kill me?" There's a quiver in my voice.

"Anyone who's a Predestined for the Veradi Council is no friend of mine."

Once again, since coming to Gahes, fear grips me. I must control it to think clearly. "You don't like the Aesir, and even less the Veradi, is that the reason?"

"For what reason should I like them? They rule Heras like lords, as if we be dogs in a kennel. While we work and suffer, Aesir gets provisions free, from their high-falutin science. And for what reason am I in this foul place if not for Veradi decreeing that I be here?"

"That's true, you have every reason to hate the Veradi for sending you here, but then, so do I! We are no different in that respect. My banishment, especially to the Geltch, shows how much the Veradi judge me an enemy. If you hate the Veradi, why kill one of their enemies?"

"You're still Aesir," he insists with vehemence.

I begin to perceive the brute Herasian thinking. The logic that 'the enemy of my enemy is my friend' does not weigh heavily with him. Paramount in his mind is emotional association. Very well, I'll attempt to fit into that pattern: "Do you know the real reason why I'm defective in Veradi eyes? It's because I was born from Herasian blood. I may have been conceived on Aesiris, but my character and temperament are Herasian. If you kill me it would be like killing a brother."

"Get this drift," he says, picking up his knife. "I'll put it simply. If I let you live after I take your kit you'll be a threat to me forever after. And I do intend to have that kit!"

Finally he has admitted his real motive. "That's too bad," I reply, making a determined effort not to show fear. "I thought I could make a deal with you."

"Eh? You, Aesir, who hardly knows how to boil water, make a deal with me?"

"Certainly. We could make a very practical team. What do you want most of all?"

"To leave Gahes," is the immediate response.

"Sure! So do I, only I know how it can be done!"

The Herasian stoops on one knee, places the knife to my throat, and asks: "How?"

"What number of vul-canae do you see passing overhead in, say, sixty days?"

"One or two."

"Good! And there are more you don't see. If we had a harmonized radiation gun we could easily knock a vul-canae out of the sky without doing too much damage to it. Then we could use it to escape."

"And how you figure it'd be easy?"

"The gun would first detect the ship by deflecting signals off it, then narrow its beam for more focused power. By varying its electro-magnetic frequency it will find a frequency that will coincide with the gravity dissipation frequency of the ship, cause harmonic distortions with that frequency and make the ship lose altitude.

"I may not know how to boil water but I do know how to

make a radiation gun. If you would provide enough food from now on for both of us, I could work on it, and within a Gahean year I estimate we'll both be on our way to Heras. With an arrangement like that I don't care if you keep my survival kit."

The knife drops from my throat. The man steps back and stares me in the face. He's making a decision. "You say if I provides for us both over the year you don't care if I keep the kit?"

"Why should I if I don't need the kit for survival?

"And you'll work on a way that gets me off Gahes?"

"That's right."

He lifts his knife again and steps toward me. Has my argument been sufficient to sway his mind, especially to beat him on his own narrow ground of self-interest? He again falls on one knee, gives me a sly look and...proceeds to cut my bonds! I have won another battle against Gahes.

"I know little about technology," he remarks, "but you convinced me you're new and had a stay in the Geltch. A man is gutsy to have your ilk, and intelligence. When someone like that gives me offer to leave Gahes, I'll take my chance. Besides, I sees a lot the Aesir can do. I warn you, though, it works. Get my drift?"

His warning is completely unnecessary since I have no intention of failing. I'm in more of a hurry than he is to leave Gahes, and I know my technical ability is sufficient to make this comparatively simple device. The main problem will be obtaining materials.

I relax my arms and legs, massaging them to encourage circulation. They've become stiff from the bonds. "Why are you so concerned about marauders? Who are they?"

"Marauders are people who come to take my turf. We're not the nicest lot on this world, you know. We'll slit each other's throat for lodging better than the one we have, or even for a few fish, if truth be told. There's no law here that says we can't."

"Now I see why you were so worried about my presence. But does everyone here live alone, in mortal fear of his neighbours?"

"A lot of us do. Others grab a woman and live with her, or they bands together in groups. They're the ones I really fear."

"Why?"

"Because they raids us loners, that's why! So far I kept this cave from their sight. They've no savvy that it be here, and I don't want a novice like you spoiling it for me."

"Why don't you join a band for protection? There's strength in numbers."

"There's things that are fixed no matter how right it seems that they be changed. I'm a loner and that's a fact. I never chimed with other folk; I always end in a row with them and I might as well spill that to you now."

His reply triggers a deep recognition that this existence on Gahes possesses a reality of life I could never find on Aesiris. Here is life lived as designed by nature, where nature is king, whose laws cannot be subverted by sophisticated intellectualizing. How primitive, thought, from the Veradi who are the complete masters of their own natures.

"Well, if we're going to be partners, what's your name? Mine is Lucirin."

"Call me Shura. It's short for Shuraz-ti Bar."

"Would you mind telling me your crime that had you banished to Gahes?"

"Murder."

I believe him.

7

ARRANA

AFTER ESCAPING THE VINE swamp there remained the formidable problems of survival, with the chance of starving or poisoning myself with an innocent looking weed. Meeting Shura was most fortunate. On the price of a promise to escape Gahes he performs the menial tasks of life, freeing my hands to work on escape.

"You want metal," he confirms as we enter a cave in the forest floor. "You'll find it, in these nodules. I smelt the copper for spears and tools." He digs a piece of malachite from the sandstone. "All you want is here, but I warn you: the marauders are all around, and if they find this mine, that finishes it for both of us. I need not tell you how sorely grieved I'll be if that happens."

A later, lone visit to the mine brings attention to heeding Shura's warning. Shouting echoes in the distance. The mine is near a ridge overlooking a rift and another ridge, the crevasse between the two ridges being deep, with high cliffs on either side comprised of nearly vertical rock. The voices come from the opposite ridge. Peering through bushes to discover the cause of the commotion, I see four marauders, with another in bondage facing the precipice. The shouting comes from the leader of the four, who appears to be wearing the claws of a beast. He raises a hand and lacerates the captive down his chest. Another marauder standing behind the victim gives him a powerful kick, careening him over the cliff. The man screams until his body splatters on the rocks below. Such is Gahean justice.

The vision of violence is with me for the rest of the day, and makes me all the more fearful of being found in the mine where I must work. The mine is well hidden, but I dare not revive the fire for fear its smoke will be detected, even though the hearth and bellows are well within the mine.

Days later I return to Shura's camp and tell him what I had witnessed. "It's the first time I've ever seen anyone killed...murdered! It was ghastly!"

"Eat the fish," he responds. "Did you eat your paste? I don't want you sick, not with the work you have to do." The 'paste' is a bacterial culture provided in my survival kit to digest the alien life-forms of Gahes.

"I ate it a long time ago. I still got a little sick. Does the food ever taste better?"

"Never. It's always bland, at least for folk. Don't know how it tastes to Gahean critters, though. Maybe to them it tastes good. Just like your rations to me. That was a feast after all these years. Too bad they're finished."

There's a long silence while I continue pecking at my fish and root-weed. The violence of the planet has affected me, and this is clearly visible to Shura. It makes him concerned. "How long you say to build that ray-gun?" he asks.

"I thought about a Gahean year. That was before I knew the marauders would be so troublesome. Now I think it'll take longer. Perhaps three years."

Shura throws his scraps into the smouldering fire in a fit of disgust. "And you reckon I'll support you with food for three years? Not likely! I'm making a change in our accord. From now on you provide too."

I have little choice since the alternative is starvation.

"Alright, Shura. But you realize the time I spend fishing and root gathering will be time taken from the project."

"Find an easier way."

"The only way is to simplify the device. I was going to include a sensor, then all we would have to do is narrow the beam to pull down a flight-ship. Without it, a lot will depend on luck."

"Just get it done," he snarls.

The new chores introduce me to more of the challenges of Gahes, from which I gain an appreciation of its many varied species. Some are a joy to hunt, like the 'flopper,' a disc shaped animal that floats on lakes and ponds, living off microbes. When disturbed, its muscular disc contracts to scoop water and force a stream from behind, that rockets the animal to a new area of its pond. They present a challenge for my fledging hunting skills, but it is not unusual for Shura to net three or four 'floppers' in one cast.

But as satisfying as it is to have my survival skills improve, still I find my eyes drifting to the night sky, searching for the sparkle that is Aesiris. How well I know its patterns, even without consciously willing to learn them; both Aesiris and Heras are planets of Kol and both are not always visible from Gahes. Aesiris is the closer to Kol, and when it appears, its amber light shinning brightly, I become restless. On those occasions I ask Shura to hunt along with him, and although he sometimes complains that I slow him down or blunder into a foolish position, more and more he seems to agree that it is a useful exercise, not only to inform me of the protein sources available but for the more practical reason, he has discovered, of teamwork.

On one hunt we are deep in the forest on the trail of what Shura calls a 'twister'. I watch the strange phenomenon: an assemblage of insect larvae bound tightly into an elongated coil about the thickness of a man's waist, stretching as much as thirty paces, undulating through the vegetation. By co-ordinated expansions and contractions of each insect with the others, the coil can move as one unit through the forest much more readily than any larva could do singly. When the coil reaches a desired spot, it disintegrates into millions of components that leave a wide area stripped of foliage, then reassembles and moves on.

We follow the 'twister' for the better part of a day, waiting for it to disperse to scoop up its delectable worms, when we chance upon grizzly evidence of atrocity. We find the remains of three men tied spread-eagle across trees, and under each of them are ashes from a fire that burned directly under their midriff. The cadavers are partially consumed by the fire, in particular their genitals.

"Rapists," Shura says. "What you see is the favorite scathe for rape."

"But who would commit such barbarity?"

"The Arransin, of course."

"Arransin! Who are they?"

"Some in their troop were raped. These were the guilty. This was their scathe, and a dire one indeed."

"The marauders rape as well as steal and murder, do they?"

"What do you think I'm telling you? These were some who did...until caught. The Arransin laid a trap for them, and it looks like they were well confused."

"I'm confused. The Arransin, who are they?"

"Women. All women - thirty, or there abouts."

"And they did this?"

"For sure. So the other marauders be a little fearful before they do their crime. But they still do, as a kind of macho fun."

"But who are those women? Where did they come

from?" I could not imagine Maiori or anyone else acting so barbarously.

"They're escapees from other bands. Women fare poorly in the bands. They're slaves, sexually and menially. The Arransin reckon they can do better on their own, which is true. But the marauders are always out to return them to their lair, so the Arransin take measures...like this."

Days later I find Shura about to leave camp, carrying a fresh catch of fish. I ask where he's going.

"I answer instinct," is his only response.

After I confirm my ignorance of instinct, he responds: "I'd hardly believe it, except from Aesir. If you want to see where I'm going you have a half day on the run."

Being curious, I agree to join him. At the end of first sun our run is complete, when Shura places his fish on his spear and carries them above his head, as if it were a sign for anyone who might see him. It isn't long before I realize we're being watched. We approach a clearing in the forest, when I turn to see several marauders following closely behind, knives drawn, wearing leather armour and painted faces. We enter the clearing where we are immediately surrounded by a troop of fighters featuring the same fierce appearance. Only then do I realize they are all women.

"Meet the Arransin," Shura says.

My Aesir status is immediately apparent to the wild throng that gathers. The women gaze wide-eyed, walk alongside, some touch but most keep a respectful distance. All have quizzical looks and giddy smiles, as if an Aesir on Gahes were the strangest anomaly. Most noticeable are their physiques, being well honed from active lives. All wear leather arm protection for firing bows, metal bands, earrings or wooden plugs, tattoos and the various paraphernalia of savages.

The camp consists of rough bivouacs constructed in a circle in the middle of the clearing, with no sign of permanency. A communal fire and pot with steaming broth are in the center of the compound. We arrived just at evening meal, which I suspect was calculated by Shura. He continues walking to one structure, oblivious to the crowd, when the curtain over the face of the approaching shelter parts and a commanding woman emerges to greet us. Her features are striking, with shoulder length hair of reddish hue and fierce eyes that give the impression of a predator about to pounce. After a moment of distrust she looks me up and down with a whimsical smile. I apparently amuse her.

"Who's this?" she asks.

Shura supports his spear with one hand, places his other hand on my shoulder and answers: "He's Aesir, Lucirin by name. I thought you'd find entertainment for him."

The woman smirks. "Let it never be said that Arrana wasn't hospitable to Aesir." She throws up the curtain to secure it on her bivouac roof, and motions me inside. "Enter, Lucirin. I'll brew some tea. We'll talk for a while and have some vitals."

"He's not just Aesir," Shura adds. "He was a Predestined for the Veradi Council. Predestined even for Rasan. Treat him well."

A murmur rolls through the crowd.

"Well, I *am* impressed," the leader of the Arransin remarks.

Before I enter, Shura breaks into quiet laughter, ill concealed behind his full beard.

The strong scent of freshly cut wood permeates the shelter's interior. The structure is too low to allow standing inside; I sit cross-legged in the Herasian manner, beside a pile of soft ferns indicating a bed. Arrana places some herbs into a clay pot, then exits to fetch hot water. She is a most shapely woman, still in her prime years but considerably older than me. Such womanly musculature combined with her predatorial features, especially those feline eyes, gives her a most alluring look.

She returns and says: "You seem nervous."

After some hesitation, I agree. "I saw your work in the forest."

"Ah!" she responds, but says nothing more about it, directly. "It's strange, you Aesir are so much against violence. You teach it's the mark of the inferior, of the animal, yet you cause so much of it...here."

I slowly nod agreement. "Of course, you realize, if you don't mind my saying so, that the people sent here are criminals, and crime by nature is violent. So the violence on the planet is caused by the nature of the people sent here."

"And a brash one you are, to say such a thing. Typical Aesir, for sure: everything so rational. Then what was your terrible crime?" She passes a clay bowl of her tea, then calls outside for two bowls of broth from the communal hearth.

"I'm here because I opposed the Belief. I've never committed a crime..." The flash of her eyes brings home the pretentiousness of my claim.

"For sure. We're all criminals...except you. In my case, I poisoned an important Herasian official. Easy it was, I worked in his kitchen. My family was indentured to him, so there was no escape. He was a brutal man, who expected intimate favors. Finally I had enough. But who was the criminal? Spend a few years on Gahes and you'll end just like us, no worse and no better.

"I think it has to do with the very nature of this place," she continues in the same sing-song Herasian brogue spoken by Shura. "Unnatural it is, at least for folk. Like the color of the plants, all black, with deep and dark shadows laying all between. It seems to breed violence. Can that be true, Master Lucirin?"

"Color is certainly important. It was color, aura color, that confirmed my banishment to Gahes."

"Then if that be true about color, the Aesir send us here not for our benefit, for you'd think our discard here be crafted to make us less violent, not more."

A band member enters with the broth. After a few sips I remark that it's the best food I've eaten on Gahes. "You have to distinguish what is Aesir from the policies of the Veradi," I respond defensively. "The Veradi have twisted and warped what is good about Aesiris to suit their own fanaticism. To justify their revered station they've become traitors to Aesiris, and to all Kolaria. But I'll deal with them in time. Someone has to, or they'll keep us all imprisoned by their rigid dogma."

"What can one person do?" she asks sceptically.

"If I had a flight-ship I'd show you. That's my first objective, to get a ship. Then head for Heras. There's discontent on that world. When I'm there I'll raise a following."

"And then what? Plant bombs? Become a nuisance?" She gives me a patronizing look, as if my ambitions were nothing more than the daydreams of a disaffected youth.

"Nothing like that. I intend to undermine the Veradi by exposing their hypocrisy and cowardice. I know that will take years, perhaps a lifetime, but I also know I'm equal to the task. I have a deep sense of destiny, and a belief it will be done as long as I try. There'll be a day of vengeance, I promise you, and when that day comes I would not want to be a Veradi."

"At least you're not short on confidence." She drinks from her soup bowl, holding it with both hands to her lips, still wearing her jocular smile. "A man with assurance about him gives cause to admire. Before anything, though, you need to leave Gahes. And how will you manage that, Master Lucirin?"

"A plan is underway. I'm working on a radiator to disable a flight-ship. Currently, though, I'm having trouble with marauders."

For the first time Arrana drops her smirk. "You have a way to leave this horrid world?" She finally takes me seriously.

"I do." I look at her appreciatively before drinking more of her tea. It has a tranquilizing effect. "But it only calls for two or three people to escape, depending on the class of ship we bring down. It'll probably be just a research vessel."

"Only you and Shura?"

"That's the plan."

"If you want more hands, we can help."

"That's not possible. There would be too many people that would attract attention, and a lot of the work only I can do."

"You fear marauders. We can help against them."

"I would prefer to avoid conflict."

"Now Master Lucirin, you're not telling me you prefer Shura's company to that of a brawny wench. There's some advantages that a woman gives, if you know what I mean."

"...Not entirely. So far Shura has been indispensable. I couldn't betray that help."

"Then you're not long on Gahes, for sure. Such loyalty deserves reward. And you were Predestined for Rasan. I never met anyone with that mark before." She shifts her position to sit closer beside me. Our bare knees touch. "Gahes becomes more dangerous, it is. The leader of the band I escaped from wears animal claws. They enforce his rule. He works not a twit. He wears them only because they can de-gut a man with one swoop." She exposes her thigh, revealing four old, parallel gashes. "Feel them, how deep they are."

I hesitantly place my fingers gently over the wounds and feel the firm, warm flesh of her thigh.

"When he did that, I left, and took some friends with me. I'm on top of his list now, for execution."

"I know who you mean."

Second sun is dipping below the horizon, leaving creeping darkness upon the camp. Shadows cast by dying embers of the outside fire caress her well-sculptured frame.

"Couldn't you find a little more room on a ship you capture?" Her fingers run through my hair. "You're such a different man from the brutes on this world. Ambitious too. I like that."

Arrana is clearly a lusty woman, with strong appetites for more than just good food. Nor does she hesitate to use her womanly charms to gain a personal opportunity. The experience is so new to me, having been raised in the totally intellectualized and emotionally sterile environment of Aesiris, the gesture is startling.

"This is your first time away from Aesiris?" Her smile is back, but no longer mocking.

"It is. I'm not familiar with Herasian customs."

"I see that. You've much to learn about life. I'll teach you Herasian ways. They're far different from Aesir. One custom we have is hospitality."

"That's a fine art on Aesiris."

"I suppose Aesir are hospitable, as much as dry fish can be, but on Heras we hardly think of it as art. There it's more like pleasure."

"Well, speaking of hospitality, I'll have to impose on yours for the night. Would you have a place in camp for guests?"

She laughs. "Like I said, Master Lucirin, I'll teach you Herasian ways. There's no special place for guests here."

"I see. Well, do you have any suggestions where I could spend the night?"

"Indeed I do." She rises to grasp the curtain still secured to the bivouac roof. It falls over the entrance, causing blackness within. "You'll stay the night here."

"Where should I sleep?

"Only one bed there is. That's our way, so the foreigner feels at home."

"We have to...share it?"

"Yes, but you say that like it's a chore. At first it'll be strange for Aesir, for sure, but don't be alarmed. We'll get along just fine."

The dark shadow of her clothing slips to the floor. She drops to her knees to throw her arms over my shoulders and lean closer. Her kiss is warm and soft. Her erect, naked breasts press my chest. Like a wild, predatorial animal she caresses, biting, licking, laughing. Her scent, her firmness, her beauty conspire to arouse Herasian instincts. My hands reach for her well rounded buttocks. I recall my chosen philosophy, that brought me to Gahes. *I have arrived.* Her strong legs wrap around my waist, and from my sitting position she draws me down. We collapse on her bed, locked in embrace.

Since that day I have revisited the camp often, bearing gifts of fish and roots as is the custom. The days of nervous shyness are gone. Arrana and I have drawn ever closer, and I have come to regard her and her followers as my most trustworthy allies.

8

ESCAPE

M PARTNERSHIP with Shura has been one of constant suspicion. If the radiation gun progressed slowly his mistrust heightened and I would have to argue at length to explain the slowness. When progress was more noticeable he became more congenial, losing his silence when at our meal of fish and roots. It was no little relief to us both when the radiator was finally completed.

The site I've chosen to demonstrate the device is a high bluff overlooking a wide expanse of sea, where the sea sweeps inward forming a shallow bay. An excellent vantage point, I wait there now for Shura, to show him the gun's operation.

As he approaches, picking his way up the rocky hillside, he quips: "You say that silly contraption gets us off Gahes? It looks tame to me. This show will have to be good before I believe it."

I switch on the gun and aim at a strategically placed tree near his path. The wood bursts into flame, sending Shura scurrying for cover. "You did want convincing," I laughingly shout back.

"Aesir ass..." Shura is still bug-eyed when he reaches the promontory, breathing deeply from exertion. "Alright, you made your point. What can it do at long distance?"

"Range makes little difference. You see that awk gliding way overhead?" Again the gun pulses. The silent predator convulses, then explodes with its blood and entrails falling out of the sky.

"In all my days I never saw a bird killed so easy." Shura is visibly impressed. "You Aesir are a strange bunch. Lucirin, I take back my suspicions. With all the delays I thought you might be feigning. If this show had no success I was ready to finish our league. Get my drift?"

Having come to know this murderous scoundrel over the past three years, his 'drift' is easily interpreted. He looks over the assembly, fingering his beard and not quite knowing what to make of it. "I still say it's silly in looks. You work it how?"

"Its operation is simple but will take some practice. By filling and emptying the lamp cylinder with air it flashes light, with the frequency modulated by adjusting the length of the cylinder. Trouble will come when the ship attempts to change its flight frequency once it finds it's a target, but its new frequency can be found by trial-and-error."

"So we aim the gun and dial the knob...at the same time. With a vul-canae in flight, that be tricky."

"Yes, it will be. I first wanted to include a self-focusing sensor, but scrapped it on your insistence to finish the project. That's the price we pay for haste. Our victim will be more difficult to bring down safely. Remember, we don't want to destroy the ship, but if you see it escaping it will have to be destroyed. We don't want survivors spreading a warning to other ships that may visit our area."

"That makes sense. I want the first look, today, right now. The chance that I finally rids myself of this place makes me all the more itchy."

"Just a little more patience, Shura. This gun won't do us the slightest good if the Aesir detect our presence, and they can do that with their cephalo-probes. I still have to make a copper helmet with simple circuitry. It shouldn't take long. You'll have to wear that helmet every time you operate the gun."

"Wouldn't you know, more delays," he grumbles.

Days pass slowly as no flight-ship is sighted. We take alternate turns at the gun, my time away from the bluff being days of relaxation, the first I have enjoyed on Gahes. The planet is not without its natural beauty, and these are days when I traverse its hills and from them gaze upon this wide water world and its far off islands, gather wild fungus that exude intoxicating scent, sate myself on tasty red bulbs hanging from the nests of buzzing insects, entertain myself from scuttling animals with twitching antennae, all the while ever mindful of the marauding danger that comes in the form of my own species.

On a sunlit evening, in a quiet glen, I assess my accomplishments. One realization stands out from my ordeals on this world: the situations when I was most challenged, if those challenges were met with fortitude and determination, were exactly the situations that strengthened me as an individual and increased my future chances of survival. By enduring the vine swamp I impressed Shura, who in turn taught me the arts of provision from raw nature. By surviving Gahes I'm now in position to threaten a flight-ship. With each challenge I have grown, certainly in craft, stealth and cunning, but most noticeably in appearance, evident from my mirrored reflection in a quiet pool. No longer am I the frail youth of Aesiris. After three years on this horrid planet, the hard work of digging, hauling, lifting, running and fighting, even in this light gravitation, has given me a vigorous physique.

Could the Veradi appreciate, inwardly and profoundly, this principle of adversity and survival in nature? Those hypocrites! Those thieves who have stolen my rightful inheritance! And such cowards! Even now they take no steps against me although they know I have survived. Their ships scout the planet with cephalo-probes telling them the presence of any individual by brain pattern identification.

My next work must be to plan my struggle with the Veradi, and for that I must know more about Heras. Anyone else in my position might use this chance to escape Kolaria, and flee into the galactic void, but I have learned well my lesson on adversity and survival. It will be used for the great day of vengeance.

One day Shura returns from his watch appearing in better humor than usual. I use our time at evening meal to press for a description of Heras as he knew that world, hoping for a hint of Veradi weakness there that I can exploit.

"What you want to know first about Herasians," he begins, "is they hate Aesir. For sure, some hate them more than others, and some are downright flunkies of Aesir. But by-and-large everyone hates them, from the lowest manure-peddler to the highest official."

"That's something I would never learn on Aesiris," I muse. "Do they rule unjustly?"

"For sure they rule unjustly. Just being our masters they deprive us. The Aesir are a scourge, who are not just foreigners, who are not just a smother of our own resolve, they be pompous fanatics who grind us under their iron Belief."

Shura reminds me of my lessons on Herasians: how they are not of sufficient calibre to accept the discipline of the Belief. Now I am learning about that Herasian rejection first-hand, from the Herasian viewpoint with which I find some agreement. Perhaps it is my own Herasian extraction that allows me to empathize with Shura's banter about freedom, for his ideals are not logical by Aesir standards. If society can be run by the sure hand of benevolence, why introduce inevitable social and political entropy with mass democracy?

"The Aesir themselves don't have democratic government,"

I reply. "They can't have, since they live by a Code, and any code must be determined by reason or doctrine, not voting."

"It bothers me not a twit what the Aesir impose on themselves. They be a different sort than we, and what suits them is no sure fit for us."

An insightful fellow, this Shura. He realizes that the despotic intellectualism of Aesir government is tailor made for people who are by temperament and training disciplined to the moral standards of a code. But it is beyond Herasians to ask what the ultimate evolutionary destiny is of their society. Could it not be one of maximum efficiency, exactly the type they now have imposed by the Aesir?

"Mostly hatred of Aesir comes from the blatant privilege," Shura continues. "If Aesir or their cursed machines were less in view there'd be less displeasure abroad. I remember one case: a wealthy Herasian who wanted to impress some backers with finery made from craftsmen. He was outdone by Aesir who only wanted to show his energy-materializer. Occurrences like that cause soreness, and they happen often."

The general weakness of Veradi rule is revealed as I listen to Shura. Being isolated from the needs of economics and survival, and having become alienated from emotion, such feelings of resentment, envy, jealousy and hate have become unintelligible to them. Living solely by the intellectual faculties of the mind, the more deeply seated, instinctual qualities of Herasians are either not understood, or are considered due to insufficient reasoning and simply dismissed. Thus the gap between rulers and ruled widens.

"There are two main cities on Heras, Quareg and Tasis. Quareg is by far the larger and has the Capitol. There you'll find most vex against Aesir, except for the wealthy class that's wholly under Veradi power. That class is loathed by all Herasians, and also the militia, because both sell the freedom of Heras for personal gain, and the Aesir reward them well."

The upper class Herasian elite of Quareg will provide most of my opposition. The Aesir do not steep themselves in the mundane affairs of ruling, leaving the secondary levels of government to Herasians after making sure their surrogates are well indoctrinated.

"Of course, the ruling class slices a small wafer, even in Quareg. Its weight far exceeds its numbers. The bulk of Quareg's litter, reckoning mostly of craftsmen and small merchants, has no succour with Aesir, and the same is true of Tasis."

"How are the country people disposed?"

"They be useless for revolt. They're too poor. From that class the militia is drawn. Take a poor youth from the fields, give him the prestige of a uniform and two hot meals each day, and he'd imprison his own mother. The country is so poor its folk grovel in awe of the wealthy. So there's just one group to reckon for revolt: the class of merchants and craftsmen. The wealthy would never chance their position while the country-folk are too submissive."

Shura's talk gives me some clues on how to begin my operations. Securing a revolutionary following should not be difficult owing to the discontent on that world. All depends on the success we have with the present plan for leaving Gahes.

As the days pass I become anxious. Finally I grow weary of a hunt and decide to join Shura at the bluff, only to find he is not at his vigil. Could he have met with an accident, or marauders? I quickly dismiss this thought. After twenty-one Gahean years he has become too cautious and wiry for anything like that to happen at a crucial time. Another, more sinister, thought occurs to me, one that is more befitting his character: *Shura has already shot down a flight-ship and has told me nothing about it!* Such a foolish scoundrel!

When I see him again I say nothing of my discovery nor does he mention anything unusual. This leaves me no choice but to keep a close eye on him, after feigning that I am dutifully leaving for my watch.

In the early part of the next Kolaster day, Shura's routine is the usual fishing while a light mist hangs over the ever placid sea. It is not until mid-morning that he carries his cooked catch into the forest, obviously on his way to a rendezvous. Stealthily following through the underbrush, I am led at first in the direction of our gun position, then around the arc of the bay towards a large cave above the shore. I follow him quietly into the cave and around a bend where the glow of a fire casts moving shadows. Voices erupt, one being obviously Shura's but the other is female, and agitated. It sounds familiar. Shura stands about a spear's throw away, and kneeling beside the fire, with a look of much distress, is...*Maiori!*

From the shadows I observe the happenings. Shura approaches her, presenting his fish and what looks like paste, but the gesture is repugnant to Maiori who has never tasted flesh. From their exchange of words it is clear that she is becoming apprehensive, and, knowing Shura, for good reason. Having rebuffed the fish offering, Shura is angered and now has full intention of forcing her to his will — Maiori, a delicate Aesir blossom at the hands of this criminal!

I step from the shadows. Shura spins around with his spear raised but recognizing me in the firelight there is a moment of hesitation. "Lucirin! You followed me here!"

"Yes, you fiend!"

"We can't allow this woman to spoil our plans!"

"My plans don't require you any more!"

"I know she's a partner of yours; she told me. I only wanted to... befriend her before I let you know what happened!"

"Don't you think I'm wise to your ways by now, you murderous rogue! You're as vile as any life on this planet! You belong here!"

Shura lunges his spear to my throat, which I parry. One nick and the poison would have me. With his spear deflected he throws his weight against me in one motion, spilling us both on the ground. We roll through the hot coals of the fire, fighting hand to hand. In the shadows a large pit comes into view - Shura is trying to manoeuvre me toward it. He attempts a kick to my groin that throws him off balance, when I give him a solid thrust towards the pit. My youthful agility has advantages. He stumbles over the edge, slips a body length down the side and manages to secure himself on an outcropping of rock. I raise a large stone above my head...

"Lucirin! No!" For the first time I hear alarm in Shura's voice. "Below me afar, in this pit, lives all the vermin of the Geltch!"

The stone connects on his head with a dull thud; his hands release their hold and the limp body arches back, into the blackness beneath. An instant of silence...then a splash and the rustle of a thousand slithering creatures. Shuraz-ti-Bar is dead.

"Oh! Lucirin!" Maiori cries. "Dare I think it is you? How you have changed!" She breaks into sobs on my chest as I try comforting her. I can hardly believe it is Maiori trembling in my arms. "Such a horrible place! And that horrid man! Take me away from here!"

"I will, Maiori. You'll be safe now that I've found you."

Maiori is a pitiful sight. There are bruises on her arms, her tunic has a tear in front, and her hair is matted with dirt. She sobs uncontrollably. Finally she raises her tear-laden eyes and manages a thin smile: "I guess you're surprised to see me."

I nod agreement.

"I was so worried when I heard what happened to you, my only thoughts were to help." She relaxes her hold as we stroll back to revive her fire. She brushes a strand of hair off her soot-smeared face. "My chance came when the Zoological Department requested volunteers for an expedition to Gahes. Because I've been working very hard at my studies since you left, I was chosen. My heart jumped when you were detected by our cephalo-probe, although I couldn't reveal my feelings to my flight companions. You've been detected by former ships also, and that has stirred concern among the Veradi."

"And well it may!" I interject scornfully. "Tell me, where are your companions, and your ship?"

"We were cruising at low altitude when our gravity fluctuated, heaving us against the ceiling. Our computer said a radiation beam was attacking us. It tried to avoid the beam but to no avail; we lost control and crashed into a nearby hill. We thought we were lucky at that point to have no one severely injured, until that vile man, Shura, crept from the forest carrying a spear. We tried to flee but he killed my two companions. He dragged me into this cave where I've been ever since...Oh! I've been so frightened and miserable here!"

"Maiori, this is important: did your ship send a distress signal?"

"Yes, of course!"

"How many days ago was that?"

"Um...Two, I think, counting today."

"Well, if relief has to come from Aesiris we'll have lots of time to repair your ship, if it isn't too badly damaged."

"No...relief won't have to come all the way from Aesiris. We passed a star-cruiser at Degras. We can expect it to rescue me."

This is alarming news since a star-cruiser is a warrior class ship directed by artificial intelligence and possessing annihilator defences that could destroy my puny radiation gun with ease. And Degras is the moon of Gahes, close enough for the ship to find Maiori by tomorrow. "Show me the wreck," I request, steeling myself against this news. "Perhaps I can still repair it in time."

Upon reaching the wreck all hope of using that twisted metal hulk is dashed. The engine is sheared and half missing — flung, most likely, into the sea. This puts me in a dilemma. I cannot simply allow Maiori to be rescued, since she would tell the circumstances of her crash and the star-cruiser would suspect my radiation gun. I could hide her from the cephalo-probe until the next ship arrived, and try again, and the star-cruiser would not know why the expedition ship crashed provided I destroy its flight memory; yet the thought of capturing a warrior class ship is tantalizing.

"You must return to the cave," I tell her. "I'm going to seek help. There's not a grain of time to spare."

"You're going to leave me? Alone? In that cave?" she asks wide-eyed.

"I'd like to take you from here, to my own shelter. The problem is time. We might already be too late. Damn that Shura! You'll be alright in the cave. You've already spent a night there, and you'll have Shura's spear that can kill the largest beasts on Gahes. It's poisoned, so never touch the blade. I promise not to be long."

I give her a long embrace and can feel the poor girl trembling. How pleasant it would be to stay with her and forget the cares of this hateful world. Yet it is that very thought that motivates me now to tear myself away. "I'll be back as soon as I can," I tell her, already pacing and hardening myself to her forlorn gaze.

My only recourse is to seek help from the only people who have provided a measure of friendship on Gahes: Arrana and her followers. Already it is mid Kolaster day, hastening my speed through the dark forest without total disregard for its dangers. At evening, before the rise of Kol, Arrana's encampment is within reach when I become careless. A twig snaps and suddenly I'm flying through the air, amid a rush of leaves and the clanging of gongs. I've sprung a trap! The wait to see my captors is not long.

"Yeaaaaah!" sounds a figure emerging from the bushes, followed by others pointing their arrows menacingly at my back, as I try, frantically from my upside-down position, to grapple with the enwinding cord around my ankle. Without warning the cord is cut, causing my plunge to the damp soil. A swarm of deadly arrows surround my prostrate form.

"Arransin, wait!" shouts one of the voices. "This is Lucirin!"

The shafts fall away.

"Why creep through the jungle, Lucirin? To violate one of us or steal our belongings?" someone asks from the crowd.

"I must speak to Arrana on the greatest urgency. It was from haste that I sprung your trap. Can't you see how much I sweat from running?"

I am carried bodily to the center of their compound to confront Arrana, and there dumped on the ground, at her feet: "If you want to leave Gahes, now's your chance," I tell her.

"A ship! What size?"

"Big! You'll need everybody, and there's no time to lose. It's coming to answer a distress call."

"Warriors!" she screams to the troop. "Don helmets and armour. We fight!"

An animated yell issues from the unruly band that had collected and heard my plea. The fighters hastily disperse into the shelters to prepare for conflict. Soon I'm once again speeding through the underbrush, leading the women to Maiori's cave. Arrana follows closely behind. Fortunately the night is clear, being the season of our present bi-solar cycle when Gahes has no night, allowing the blaze of Kol to light our way. Shortly before Kolaster sunrise the cave is reached; its interior is dark except for the glowing embers of Maiori's fire. Maiori awakens from a light sleep: "Are these your friends, Lucirin? They look ferocious!"

"They promise to help. Now we must set a trap. The light of Kolaster is already breaking."

Arrana, indicating Maiori, scowls: "You said nothing about this useless flower. And what is this about a trap?"

A member of the band enters the cave in a run: "Leader, there's the wreck of a vul-canae not far off. Recent it is, and has the sign of the Veradi."

Again indicating Maiori, Arrana asks: "Veradi?"

"She's a Predestined."

"And this ship that comes: It's a warrior type?"

"It is."

Arrana points rigidly at me, her eyes shrivelled into narrow slits. "You've tricked me, you slithering sorlum!" she screams.

"If I had told you it was a warrior ship, would you have come?"

"Certainly not! I'm no fool to pit arrows against annihilators!"

"Yes, you would be a fool to attempt that - without me! As an Aesir myself I'm knowledgeable on their sciences, and what is offered you now is more than freedom from Gahes. I offer you wealth and fame throughout all Kolaria. But the risks are greater. Come outside and I'll reveal my plan."

Light from Kolaster is becoming strong and already burning off the morning mist. A spot must be chosen in view of
the bluff where the radiation gun is perched. The troop with
Maiori follows me to a rocky point.

"Stay here and form a circle around Maiori with your arrows, as if you were menacing her. The Aesir will isolate themselves with a projected time alteration field, by which means they
will move rapidly but to them you will appear nearly paralyzed.
This will be their protection, so *do not* make any threatening
gestures when that field is operating. You won't stand a chance.
Otherwise, don't be afraid. They won't take your lives except as
a last resort if their field should fail. That failure is what I intend
to cause, and when that happens you must be ready to strike."

"And what will be *your* part in the commotion?" Arrana
asks.

"I'm going to cause it, from the near bluff where I have a
radiation gun. It's also a weapon to be used against the ship if
the plan fails. If you wish, I can demonstrate its power."

"How absolutely generous of you, to allow us to risk ourselves and do the dirty work," she responds sarcastically.

"There's no time for arguments," I plead. "You ought to
consider this opportunity a privilege. Those who have no stomach for it, let them depart, but let them also understand they
forfeit their chance of leaving this hell-world."

A murmur of confused discontent stirs the crowd.

"It's agreed," Arrana shouts, raising her bow, "provided
Lucirin works the device he says is in his possession."

"That I can easily do. I must now leave. Don't forget your
instructions."

"One thing more. We gag and bind your friend. I've no assurance whose side she's on, ours or Aesir, and one word from

her when the ship lands could cost all our lives, except yours, of course."

I had hoped Arrana would make this demand and gesture my approval. If Maiori is made helpless it will relieve her from the burden of split loyalty and guilt.

Shortly I'm back on the bluff with my constructed weapon, that has already proved itself capable, in the hands of Shura, of affecting a vul-canae. I'm certain if the Aesir use a time alteration field against the Arransin I can destroy that field, as both gravitational and time alteration capabilities depend on the same mechanisms. Not forgetting the copper helmet if I am not to be detected by the ship's cephalo-probe, I remove the camouflage from the gun and prepare for Arrana's demonstration. With the morning mist dissipated, the band can be clearly seen across the bay, and a demonstration should not be difficult. My target will be some dried logs that have drifted onto the spit of shore where the Arransin wait. That should kindle their enthusiasm. I take deliberate aim when....

Off in the distance a bright speck catches my eye. It moves fast, high over the horizon. The object looms larger; there's now no doubt, I can see our vul-canae, and a beautiful warrior ship it is. The moment for which I've prepared so long is at hand!

Swiftly, like a swooping predator, it approaches the narrow jut of land with its landing tripod emerging from its flat belly. Arrana's followers are clearly nervous; there seems to be confusion among them, which has not been helped by not having received my demonstration. A figure emerges from the ship; its movement is fast and jittery. As I thought, the Aesir are protecting themselves with a projected time field. Events are working well so far, if the Arransin will not fear to attack when the field is lifted. I aim down the Aesir throat, ready to fire. Another figure emerges, then another and another, all wearing fearsome death helmets and staying close to the ship: Herasian guards which makes Arrana's position more dangerous. Two Aesir emerge and walk rapidly towards Maiori, their motion distorted by the time field. I must act quickly. Deciding now or never, I fire directly at the ship, destroying its protective time field projected for its occupants now on the shore. Arrana and her followers act instinctively, seeing the enemy's normal motions. The four Herasian guards are first to fall, their screams reaching my ears. The two Aesir approaching Maiori are next to succumb under a hail of arrows. Others of the band attack the ship, lunging toward its portal. The 'crack' of annihilators punctuates the commotion and now the high pitched screams of dying Arransin mingle with the cries of Herasians. I ready to destroy the ship if it cannot be taken. As suddenly as it began the commotion ends; Arrana stands at the portal and waves her arms overhead in my direction. The Arransin are efficient killers.

I run back to the site, leaving the gun operating. Upon return I'm met with the appalling spectacle of dead and dying Aesir, Herasians and Arransin, the latter having their mutilated bodies strewn over the beach. Arrana has lost half of her fighters to the deadly Aesir weapons. Quickly I enter the ship, place the ship control circuits on neutral, at the same time switching to manual. I then request that a member be sent back to turn off the radiation gun, whom I instruct on the procedure.

I next turn my attention to Maiori who still lies gagged and bound among the twisted cadavers, sick from fright. Never before has she seen death, or violence of any sort, yet in her few short days on Gahes she has been preoccupied with nothing else. How we Aesir are a sheltered lot from the realities of brute life! I undo her bonds and carry her into the ship, to a resting station.

Arrana gives her a contemptuous scowl. "Congratulations!" she says to me, well pleased. "We've captured a fine ship."

The ship is indeed magnificent, far better than I ever imagined capturing with my radiation gun. A simtal series two warrior class, it is built to carry twelve active people with provisions for twice as many. There are probes and sensors of various types, the ship has superior speed to most vul-canae, and is armed as well.

But most impressive is the ship's computer, a finely tuned oberin-series quantum tunnelizer with dual-routed targeting and speech interfaces. I've looked over the schematics of such computers, but never before have I had the opportunity to test the capabilities firsthand. I will have to be careful with this mind; it is not designed to learn or think as a human being, as many robotic servants are, but is instead designed to excel at serving its masters with maximum efficiency. A ship controlled by such a computer could be a powerful tool, but mishandled it could bring disaster on us all.

A few minor repairs from the skirmish are made while the mortally wounded of Arrana's followers are poisoned, as is the custom among the Arransin, tears are shed and the bodies of all fallen comrades cremated in a gesture of respect. Later in the afternoon we lift off the beach, amid cremation fires still pouring their smoke into the air. "Our first objective will be to destroy my radiation gun. It's best to keep the Aesir guessing on how this ship was taken." Flying over the rocky bluff, the whole spot, rock and metal, is vaporized by annihilator.

Arrana gibes: "Don't you feel at home, giving orders like a true Aesir."

"I'm the only one in this company who knows how to run this ship, what it can do, how to care for it and its limitations. It's only reasonable that I be in command."

"Let's get our positions straight," she demands, her eyes narrowing. "You command the ship, I command the Arransin."

"That's fine with me, Arrana." My amused grin holds her fierce stare.

The full weight of their accomplishment had not been immediately felt by my newly acquired comrades, who only half believed my scheme for leaving Gahes, who until this morning were resigned to a life on this world. Now, when they see the destructive power in their hands, when they witness the landscape fleeting past, jubilance erupts. "Victorious Lucirin. Victorious Lucirin," they chant. Even Arrana, despite her jealous hurt over Maiori, has a wild look of admiration in her eye. Again I am reminded of my lesson on adversity and survival. Having ventured to capture a vul-canae I have captured one of magnificence and power beyond the intention of my capture device, and have become a hero among a warrior band of criminal women that seems destined to be my loyal following.

9

HEIMBAL

"COMPUTER, give full details on last mission."

"PERSONAL PARAMETERS UNIDENTIFIED, INFORMATION CLASSIFIED, GIVE NATURE OF COMMAND."

"Not a very hospitable fellow, are you?"

"0-7-1, SIMTAL SERIES TWO, IS MY IDENTIFICATION. DETAILS ON LAST MISSION ARE OUT OF THE QUESTION."

"Well, that leaves me only one recourse." I dismantle the computer's front panelling, exposing its numerous neural pods. The curious Arransin gather around. "Our friend has to have its imprinting changed, to be loyal to us rather than to its former masters."

"WAIT! THAT WILL NOT BE NECESSARY."

"I'm sorry, 0-7-1. You're not trustworthy, and that's a fault no commander can tolerate from his ship." Turning to the Arransin: "This is a drastic surgery that will require some time, so first we'll strike a course, manually, for Degras."

"Degras!" Arrana exclaims. "Why go there?"

"Curiosity. I happen to know this ship was stationed there before it came to rescue Maiori. I want to know why a ship of this class would be interested in what is supposed to be a perfectly dead moon."

The computer imprinting is an intricate task. Facial, body and voice pattern analyses of people designated to operate the computer have to be made, or 0-7-1 will not respond to command. Instead, it will be our most dangerous enemy. I make these analyses for myself and Arrana, the hierarchy of command override in that order. A skeleton staff guides the ship, after some instruction, leaving my hands free to do the work. While making the changes members of my crew are always present, leaning over me or stretched out on the cabin floor, watching with rapt fascination the patterns of lights dancing amid the shadows of our chamber, and wondering at the sophistication displayed in the bowls of a 0-7-1 class computer. Other members of our company rest, especially Maiori who is exhausted from her Gahean ordeal.

Finally the new cells are completed, carefully placed into the proper circuit pods, and I again ask of the ship's previous mission.

"CAPTAIN LUCIRIN, IT IS A PLEASURE TO MAKE THE ACQUAINTANCE OF SO CAPABLE A TECHNICIAN." Flattery? Is the computer sincere or is it trying to distract me while trying to circumvent my reprogramming? "YES, YOU'RE RIGHT ABOUT DEGRAS. THAT WAS MY MISSION UNDER CAPTAIN BECIN. IT WAS A SIMPLE MISSION: TO QUARANTINE DEGRAS AGAINST THE ATTENTIONS OF ANY WAYFARERS."

"Quarantine! You mean that airless rock can harbour a disease?"

"A DISEASE IT IS, OF SORTS. DEGRAS IS THE LAST REFUGE OF HEIMBAL, A FORMER TETRARCH OF HERAS WHOSE PHILOSOPHY THE VERADI CONSIDER A THREAT OF THE HIGHEST MAGNITUDE TO KOLARIA, AND EVEN TO THE GALAXY. HEIMBAL HAS CONSTANTLY ATTEMPTED TO SPREAD HIS PHILOSOPHY, AND HIS INFLUENCE, FROM HIS PRESENT LOCATION. THUS THE NEED TO ISOLATE DEGRAS FROM POTENTIAL FOLLOWERS."

0-7-1 is responding well to my questioning. If it wished to deceive me it would not likely reveal this surprising information. Perhaps my suspicions are inordinate, but I must make certain this sophisticated and possibly devious machine can be trusted. "I'm familiar with the philosophy of Heimbal myself, but that philosophy is ancient. Surely Heimbal has been dead a long time."

"THAT IS THE THOUGHT THE VERADI WISH TO PERPETUATE. ACTUALLY, THERE ARE NO RECORDS OF HIS CAPTURE, AND HIS DEATH HAS MERELY BEEN ASSUMED FROM THE LENGTH OF TIME INVOLVED. HE WAS TRACED TO DEGRAS WHERE HE DISAPPEARED, EVEN FROM OUR MOST SENSITIVE CEPHALO-PROBES, AND FROM THE TIME OF THAT DISAPPEARANCE THE MOON'S SURFACE HAS EXHIBITED STRANGE OCCURRENCES."

The sound of voices disrupts Arrana and her followers from their sleep. All except Maiori enter the ship's dimmed control chamber to be within easier listening range. Their rustic appearance seems anomalous amid the technical sophistication of numerous probes, indicators and controls. Arrana wearily reclines on a flight-deck reposer.

"What strange occurrences?" I ask.

"DEGRAS HAS NEVER BEEN THE MOST CONGENIAL OF WORLDS FOR HUMAN HABITATION, BEING WITHOUT ATMOSPHERE, BUT IT WAS NOT A DEATH TRAP WHEN ONE PREPARED FOR IT," the machine drones in its monotone. "SINCE THE DISAPPEARANCE OF HEIMBAL NO ONE EMPLOYED IN THE VERADI'S SERVICE CAN STEP ON THE SURFACE WITHOUT TRIGGERING A TREMBLING OF ROCK WITH FISSURES THAT OPEN UNDER HIS FEET, AND VOLCANISM THAT SPEWS JETS OF GAS HOT ENOUGH TO MELT A PERSON ALIVE. IT IS AS THOUGH THE WHOLE SEISMIC NATURE OF THE MOON WERE UNDER INTELLIGENT CONTROL, CAPABLE OF SELECTIVE MANIFESTATION AT ANY POINT."

Arrana is still blurry-eyed from sleep. "Who's Heimbal?" she asks.

"Heimbal was once a powerful Herasian leader," I answer. "He fell into disfavor with the Veradi because he dared to question the Belief and collected a following to his own philosophy. His reign was a time of revolt against Aesiris, followed by a period of persecution when the Veradi regained the upper hand.

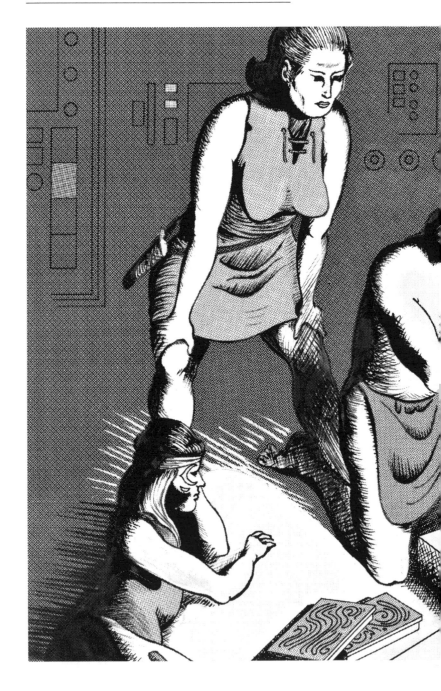

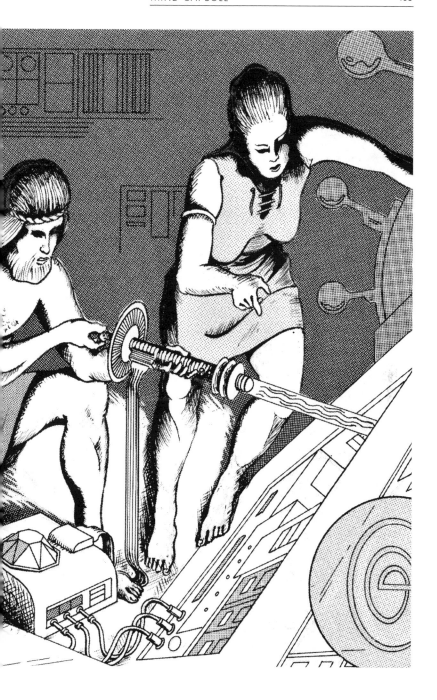

His rule must have been a popular one, judging from the tenacity of his teachings, apparently to this day."

She yawns: "I lived the first nineteen years of my life on Heras but I never heard of any Heimbal or his philosophy."

"IT'S NOT LIKELY THAT YOU WOULD," 0-7-1 explains. "THE SECT OF BALAM, AS HEIMBAL'S BELIEF IS CALLED, IS TODAY ENTIRELY UNDERGROUND AND TRANSMITTED BY SELECT PEOPLE WHO LIVE FOR THE DAY OF A FUTURE REVOLT. THE VERADI TAKE PAINS TO SEARCH OUT SUCH PEOPLE TO DESTROY BALAM FOR ALL TIME. YOU WOULD ONLY HAVE HEARD OF HEIMBAL OR BALAM IF YOU WERE INVOLVED IN THAT CONSPIRACY. OBVIOUSLY YOU WERE NOT."

The air of our now cramped chamber begins to grow warm from the presence of Arrana's followers, not being designed for so many bodies. A member, Ologa by name, speaks up: "Captain, I am of Balam. For that I was exiled to Gahes."

"Then you may be useful when we reach Degras," I reply, and return my questioning to 0-7-1: "What are the Veradi doing to handle their problem on Degras?"

"NOTHING VERY ACTIVE, EXCEPT, AS I SAID, TO ISOLATE THE MOON FROM ALL WHO PASS BY, WHICH CONSISTS OF VUL-CANAE EN ROUTE TO AND FROM GAHES. IT'S A BORING JOB AND THE VERADI BELIEVE THE SITUATION IS WELL IN HAND. THERE ARE NO OTHER SHIPS STATIONED THERE."

Our conversation shakes the sleep from Arrana, who, with the thought of danger, is stirred to sit at the edge of her reposer. She motions her head in the direction of 0-7-1's speaker: "How do you know we can trust this pile of metal?"

"We'll all know very soon," I reply since 0-7-1's voluntary information has convinced me its new imprinting is successful. "I'm going to return the ship to computer control. When still on Gahes I isolated the ship's controls from the computer and placed them on manual. Those controls included the self-destruct mechanism. If there's a mistake in the new imprinting 0-7-1 will self-destruct."

I punch the key pattern taking our flight-ship off manual and placing it back under computer control. We wait tense moments while the more efficient take-over is felt throughout, as though the ship were returning to life.

"RELAX, CAPTAIN. THE NEW IMPRINTING IS MOST SUCCESSFUL. I AM YOUR SERVANT."

A sight of relief issues throughout the control chamber.

Under computer control, the trip to Degras passes swiftly. Maiori, who has regained some of her old spirit and vitality, upon reaching Degras sits on the viewer table to watch the surface approach. "Something mysterious seems to pervade this moon, Lucirin. Just looking at the place makes my flesh crawl. You don't plan a landing there, do you?"

She was the first to feel the strange sense of foreboding that becomes stronger as we draw closer to that dark orb. The intensity of the feeling has no rational explanation, yet it is real and begins to have a telling effect on the crew.

"We must. I'm anxious to make contact with the followers of Balam, if it is they who cause the aberrations on the surface as explained by 0-7-1. They could be very useful allies when we reach Heras."

"Tell me more about Balam. You did some extensive studies of it when on Aesiris, didn't you?" She dovetails her fingers between her knees as she drapes her legs over the table's edge. A fresh tunic from ship's stores and leisurely bath helps replenish her beauty that I knew on Aesiris. How strange that we should be thrown together in these circumstances, amid the utilitarian mechanisms of a warrior star cruiser.

"I did. It was one of my activities that alarmed the Veradi."

"You always were a radical."

"Independent thinker is what I call myself. But I never thought that deciding my own views would get me into trouble, not on Aesiris, and not into *such* trouble. Imagine the injustice! All because I explored a philosophy other than the Belief."

"I warned you it would happen."

"Yes, my opinion of the Veradi was idealistic. Perhaps that's why my opinion of them has been totally reversed. I now see them as hypocrites because they supposedly revere science but have closed minds, and also as cowards because they would send me to die rather than face a challenge."

"I have to agree, their sentence was severe. But you have to consider their point-of-view. Their concern is Aesiris, the empire, society and the total collective of Kolaria. They don't look at life from the subjective view-point of any individual."

"Well, I do. After all, we are all individuals, are we not? That's why I find the philosophy of Heimbal so satisfying. The message of Balam is freedom, individual freedom, to take all restrictions off people to allow them to live a natural life. All species are born from nature and it is only through nature that they can find ultimate fulfilment."

"Ah! I see why the Veradi are so adverse to that philosophy. It's contrary to their view that we must master nature, including our own natures. It suggests that the whole purpose and mission of the Belief is a mistake."

"Exactly, and it's a point-of-view I'm wholly in sympathy with. Maiori, the time I spent on Gahes taught me more about life than the Veradi could ever reveal with all their clinical, capsulate learning."

"That's fine, but you realize as human beings we must be motivated by more than animal concerns."

"A LANDING LOCATION HAS BEEN SELECTED, CAPTAIN. I RECOMMEND THAT THE SHIP MAINTAIN LEVITATION WHILE YOUR PARTY IS ON

THE SURFACE."

I choose four people for the exploratory expedition, Arrana included and also Ologa, the Balam disciple, leaving 0-7-1 in self-command. This will be its ultimate test of loyalty. Maiori remains on board but was not imprinted into the machine's circuitry.

Degras is a dead world, requiring pressure suits that feel confining. After latching on her helmet, Terana, one of my companions, immediately tears it off. "I can't breathe in there!" she complains.

I must explain to these Herasians that such reactions are merely psychological. Although true, the gesture is indicative of the unexplainable fearfulness that grips us, that has become a critical factor among the Herasians with our approach to this moon.

We four members of the expedition party practice using our hard-shell suits, check our indicators, evacuate hissing air from our pressure chamber, and open the ship's bottom portal. The circular door rises easily on its hinge, allowing us to observe the dead world below.

"We jump from this height?" Arrana asks. The ship maintains levitation at a fearful distance above the surface, in respect for the geological anomalies forewarned by 0-7-1.

"Don't worry, just watch."

We throw seismological equipment through the floor portal and watch it gently drift down to the barren surface. My intention is to use it to detect living chambers at the moon's core. It raises a small dispersion of dust with its impact.

Arrana backs away from the floor portal. "A machine isn't the same as folk."

"You saw how slowly it fell. We'll fall the same. We won't be hurt."

"It's a devil world, this one."

"I know what your problem is, with all of you. There's something strange going on in our minds, that's making us afraid. I feel it too. But think rationally, and for once in your lives try to overcome your emotions. Neither the ship nor we can detect anything that can harm us. Are we going to flee, afraid of our shadows?"

I plunge through the portal in hope of shaming my companions; then from the surface watch their hesitant motions as they float one by one from the ship's belly.

A ship's viewer cannot do justice to a sight; one must be immersed in a scene bodily to properly appreciate nature's majesty. Apart from the brilliant globe of Gahes filling a quarter of the star-lit sky, the immediate impression of Degras is one of complete and utter desolation. A thick mantle of dust blankets the surface. Huge rocks are strewn in every direction. Craggy peaks catch the blaze of two suns, pointing their jagged fingers into the black eternity. No dust clouds linger at our feet, reminding us with every step that without our pressure suits we would explode in the vacuum around us and turn into a clinker of ice before the eyes of our companions. But most chilling is that unexplainable sensation of imminent danger, and without warning the terrain begins trembling. Great cracks open, rocks fall into the gaping fissures with gushes of frozen powder spewing skyward, boulders tumble from cliffs...

"0-7-1, how extensive is this quaking?" I ask our ship by radio.

"IT IS VERY LOCALIZED, CAPTAIN, JUST IN THE IMMEDIATE VICINITY OF YOUR SEARCH PARTY, AS I WARNED YOU WOULD HAPPEN," is the answer in my earphone.

We stagger from the trembling; two of my party fall from lack of balance. Arrana screams into my communicator: "Lucirin, this world is alive! It devours us all! Call the ship to our rescue!"

Another Herasian pleads: "Please, Lucirin, we are about to be crushed!"

"The falling rock makes rescue too hazardous to the ship. No world can be alive. This is caused by someone - someone belonging to Balam."

With that Ologa, the Balam disciple, separates from the group: "Heimbal would not scathe his children!" She then repeats a gesture, first placing her open palm on her chest, then with her palms together raises both over her head and bows from the waist. This she does over and over.

The trembling subsides. Such fortune that a follower of Balam was on the ship! The possibility seemed remote, but such is my fate that luck is forever with me.

The agitated movements of my Arransin companions now halt in astonishment for the sight that unfolds before us: over the crest of a small hill the figure of a man appears, a man who wears no protective clothing, being dressed in a long tunic, who leaves no trace of his passage in the dust under his feet. His build is lean, his face long and trails a thin, black moustache. "Am I deceived that a ship of the Veradi carries, free, one of my faithful?" the figure inquires.

Can this be Heimbal?

The Herasian follower runs over to him: "Heimbal! In gratitude and servitude I kneel before you."

The phenomenon is a technological wonder. Unlike the Herasians who accept the spectacle without question, it is clear to me that what we see cannot be the physical existence of a man who lived centuries ago, and even if the ancient tetrarch had accomplished such a feat of longevity, no manner of living being could exist unshielded against this environment of Degras. Another explanation must be sought, one possibly dealing with the ancient arts of image projection, although there is no evidence of the required devices.

The all-pervading sense of dread leaves. Now a solution to this mystery unfolds. Both the figure and the emotion are manifestations of the same field. We are in the grip of telepathized thought, that can take command of one's senses. The image before us is a phantom, a figment of our collective imaginations.

The Herasian continues: "The ship that brings me, oh persecuted one, is no longer an instrument of the hated Veradi. It was captured under Lucirin, rebel Aesir, who also stands here before you."

"Salutations, Grand Master." I step forward from the group. "I too am learned in your teach..."

"Long have I waited for this moment of physical contact from the outside, but never did I think it would come in the very ship that was my jailer. Welcome, all of you, into the realm of Heimbal. Go yonder to the largest mountain on the horizon. There you'll find an entrance. Take it." On saying this the figure vanishes as mysteriously as it came.

Strange, now, how the sensation of dread and fear is replaced by an equally intense euphoria. I swim in delight, gaiety and laughter. The abyss that my companions and I have fallen into, upon entering a cave in Heimbal's mountain, gives not the slightest consternation. Down we tumble in what seems an endless plunge. A light at the end of this long descent illuminates a tiled floor bathed in the warmth of yellow hues. We drop gently. The drunken stupor clears.

Once again Heimbal is in our presence, still and sombre, standing at a distance against the entrance of a darkened corridor. "Remove your pressure suits. Here in my domain you have safety." The apparition has its arms folded into oversized sleeves. The only motion is on its lips. Upon removing our helmets, it says: "And now introductions. Who is the leader of yon star-cruiser?"

Of course. Heimbal must rely on conventional means to *receive* communication, hence this invitation into his personal realm. Again I step forward and introduce myself.

"Lucirin, you are a man of substance. Welcome to the abode of Heimbal. My apologies for the inconvenience on the surface."

"Was that your doing?" I ask, thinking that those near calamities were also mere imagery, an idea quickly dispelled by Heimbal:

"For sure. The quaking of terrain was my directive. Not a rock falls that I don't see. But, unless you are a spy, you have little concern with such matters. What is the purpose of your mission?"

"None other than to meet your Eminence," I reply, still removing my suit. "We have common cause: to undermine the Veradi. I wish to place myself at your disposal and join your followers on Heras, to help gain their freedom and mine."

"A most noble intention. Naturally you want to know who those followers are." He is suspicious.

"The information would facilitate my work. However, if you feel I'm unworthy of your trust we can part company and I'll leave you to your solitude."

"Ach! A man of your talents be an asset, Lucirin. On the whole I deal with a pack of dolts! And I have means to see that you are in fact an enemy of the Veradi and their cursed Belief. Very well, I'll give you access to one disciple. He'll make provisions for you. That's the best I can impart under the conditions, due to respect for my flock."

"I understand." At least I am assured of one contact on Heras. Being thus satisfied, my interest turns to this enigmatic figure: "I'm impressed with your capabilities. Of course, I cannot accept you as do the simple Herasians."

"I'd be suspicious if you pretended different." Heimbal's moustache veils a wry smile. "How do you accept me?"

"With admiration, not adoration. I am a student of your teachings, but I consider you only that, a teacher, not a god. As for your present, er...state, obviously you have some marvellous technology at your disposal, being, as you are, a master of the senses."

"Follow me," he says, turning into the darkened corridor behind him. Free from the encumbrance of my space suit, I am guided by the ghostly, gliding figure into a circular compartment where rows of instrumentation encircle a crystalline machine. Levers at the machine's base move with life-like motion as the whole apparatus slowly revolves on a floor disc. Light shines from within, sufficient to bathe the chamber in its golden glow. A silver, spherical object rests at the machine's center.

"You have experienced firsthand the power of my illusions and my mastery over the world of the senses. Unfortunately, as you see, my own sensuality is somewhat curtailed."

I am aghast at his remark. The machine before me is all that is left of the master tetrarch. During the period of persecution by the Veradi he foresaw his end and prepared here his refuge, where he transcribed his thought and character into the machine's molecules. By making a total duplication of his brain he has become, for all practical purposes, immortal, surviving long after the decay of his physical body. *How ironic that the mind of our greatest teacher in the ways of natural life should be housed in a computer!*

"Kolaria dwells in ignorance of my days on Heras," he explains. "We had our technical achievements too, and life was better than now. You see, I had in that day my Aesir disciples, rebels like you, who under my governance provided powerful means to extend my influence."

"It was they who gave you the devices for telepathic hypnosis and thought field projection?"

"For sure. Actually, hypnotic control always be integral to Balam."

"A remarkable achievement. The technology I see here is most advanced, and for those times..."

"Ach, Friend Lucirin, this is Degras, not Heras. For sure some ideas are long lived, but there is little here owed to Aesiris." A light from the computer strikes my face. "Look into the beam and I'll convey to your mind a sight that is here."

The light is bright, requiring my eyes to become accustomed. It reveals two large bodies, alien bodies, about three times human size, lying motionless. The room where they lay is dark and hollow, silent as a tomb, and cold.

"They're dead. Physically dead in every way, yet in perfect preserve. Where they're from I know not. I only know because of them I live."

Thus it is by an *alien* science that Heimbal's cerebral existence continues, a formidable feat in itself, but so sophisticated is the giants' technology that they have made an entire world the realm of one mind, as if all Degras were the physical embodiment of Heimbal. "Were they followers of yours?" I ask. "Was that why they built this refuge for you?"

"No, they had no league with any philosophy or teaching. They were space wanderers. They followed their own path, whatever that was. Only by good fortune, or patient waiting on their part, I know not which, our lives crossed exactly when I needed help the most, that was when my fortunes with the Veradi went into decline. All of us, perhaps, were fleeing something; I from the dour resolve of the Veradi, and they from pur-

suers beyond Kolaria.

"Does this satisfy your curiosity about my stay on Degras?"

The light fades. "Oh...Yes!" I'm still in wonderment at the sight. "It's a pity they're not alive. We could learn much from them."

"Yes," Heimbal states matter-of-factly. "Now I'll return you to your friends."

Clearly there is more of a mystery here than Heimbal pretends, but I keep silent and ask no more questions, fearing I would appear too curious and raise his ire. That two aliens should traverse the galaxy, requiring millennia, to die on Degras yet allow the personage of Heimbal an artificial survival with no gain to themselves, is unlikely. If they were not believers of Balam, why would they go to the trouble of providing Heimbal with such an elaborate refuge? Could it be that this phantom of a man I see before me is actually the guardian of some deep secret, that this once famous and revered Heimbal is now in the service of alien powers? If so, it is in the service of those powers that I, too, am now placed.

We return to the Herasians, who again under the spell of euphoria are laughing and frolicking in a recess of Heimbal's cavern. Arrana sees me and approaches in an obviously amorous mood, having divested herself of all clothing. "We were waiting for you."

Heimbal suggests: "Enjoy some relaxation in payment for your ordeal on Degras and for the aid you are yet to provide."

With that I become overpowered by the delight of drunken abandonment. The scent of jasmine is in the air with the force of Heimbal's emotion field making its full impact on my senses. Scenes of erotica drift before my eyes. Heimbal is unquestionably a master of emotion.

"Your follower of Balam will come with me," he adds. "I have instructions for her before your party leaves."

How long before we are again on board our flight-ship I have no idea, nor can I remember leaving the abode of Heimbal. On return, the remaining crew is full of questions, in particular Maiori. On learning of our revelry she begins to have a new perception of me: "I thought you merely considered alternative philosophies," she says, arms folded. "Do you now reject so completely Aesir knowledge that you embrace Balam in spirit and deed - an ideology based on gratification of the senses?"

"Of course not," I insist. "I merely object to Veradi fanaticism. I am not of Balam. I could not resist Heimbal's emotion field. No one can. You should have experienced it too. It might have done you some good."

Although it is clear to me that Maiori, like any devoted Aesir, denies herself the appeal of natural life, I can also appreciate her perspective on Herasians. To see them through her eyes they are people enslaved by their impulses, lacking in intellectual qualities and possessing no goals loftier than those dictated by their appetites.

Our next course is straight for Heras, a tedious journey requiring hibernation for all. The expedition to Degras has gone well, for I've received what I wanted: someone on Heras to contact who can provide cover against the ruling gentry. There is only one irritation: the Balam disciple, Ologa, who has received a package of unknown contents from Heimbal with instructions on how to care for the parcel and on what to do after reaching Heras. A character change has come over Ologa since her meeting with Heimbal. She is under an intense inducement to give undistracted care to the parcel. So it is that the hand of Heimbal reaches into our ship with the placement of a Balam devotee in our midst, who carries a package with contents unknown to anyone on board and instructions that will determine our fate on Heras.

After securing the ship for our hibernation I relax in my capsule, instruct 0-7-1 to waken everyone on approach to Heras, close my canopy, and fall into...the...sleep....

10

RESPITE

BUT THE SLEEP was not the usual refreshment of oblivion. Consciousness was still there, only an inner consciousness, not of the world around. Or was a peculiar dream occurring? Time would soon give the answer, as the swirls of cloud had a direction, a purpose that one need only float upon for fulfilment of an immediate destiny. Gradually it all pulled together. A curved roof focused through the haze of swirling mass, and Lucirin became a memory, a memory of another person. Doctor Niemeyer was awakening.

The frail man lay drained of energy, his clothes soaked from sweat and excitement. He took a minute to convince himself that this was reality, not the dream he had just left, so real was its experience. Natural light entered from the porthole above and mixed with the artificial light surrounding him. Staring up blankly into those rays, his mild amnesia melted away to a slow recollection of events from the previous night: his location on the Bolivian plateau, his colleagues, and above all, the mysterious copper dome.

He tried raising himself off the hard surface. His muscles strained. The most he could manage was an arched chin in the air. A dull, aching sensation gnawed in his head with the aborted motion; every brain-cell had been worked to its limit. He collapsed back again, waited a moment, then shifted his feet to the edge and rolled onto his side. From that position he pushed himself off the 'sarcophagus' he had been lying upon, his legs first tumbling to the floor.

He crouched on his knees against the crystal, relaxed again and felt some strength return, then remembering the silver tiara, slipped it off his head. *What had he experienced? How long had he been lying there?* He could not bring his mind to focus. His overriding concern was to rest or he could start hallucinating.

Slowly he gained some balance, then stiffly tried to raise himself through the porthole in the copper roof overhead. Two pairs of strong hands grasped his wrists and hoisted him up through the hole. Cool air of the sunlit morning bathed his face and filled his lungs.

"Doctor Niemeyer!" Boyd exclaimed. "You look exhausted!"

"Oh! Good morning...Sidney...Charlie. Thanks for the hand up. Apparently I've spent all night in there, and you're right, I *am* tired."

The three men, Doctor Niemeyer, Sidney Boyd and Charlie Ryan, strolled back to their camp. Doctor Niemeyer refreshed himself with a quick face wash, changed his clothes and joined his friends at the open-air breakfast table. There, he found Leslie and Mark Jennings who made the same exclamations as Boyd at the dome. The doctor sat next to Leslie on the elongated bench of the table; Boyd and Ryan sat opposite him. The aroma of brewing coffee was in the air and delighted his nostrils.

"I'm sorry to have caused this concern," the doctor apologized. "I didn't mean to stay in there as long as I did; events just took over."

"Have you unlocked the secret of that empty shell?" Boyd queried.

"I certainly have, Sidney, and it's by no means an empty shell. It's the most amazing time capsule I ever thought possible. You might call it a *mind capsule.* I'll tell you all about it once I'm my old self again."

"Can't you tell us anything, Doctor?" Boyd insisted. "We're all dying with curiosity."

"Well, I'll try. You know that oblong, box-like structure in the center, that we thought was a 'sarcophagus'...?"

"Yes?"

"It's a...memory...transcriiiiber...." Doctor Niemeyer's head gently rolled onto the shoulder of the girl sitting next to him.

"A memory...what?" the two men seated opposite him at the table exclaimed in unison.

"Save your breath," Leslie said. "He's asleep."

Doctor Niemeyer slept through the rest of the day, waking toward evening with the sounds of camp dinner being prepared. He ate a hot meal and at last chatted with his companions on the night's experience. After relating the whole story he commented: "It's all so real! I remember every incident as if it happened to me personally: the magnificence and grandeur of Aesiris, the complex technology, the cold demeanor of the Veradi, the wild terror of Gahes. It's all now part of my memory as though it happened to me in reality and not some ancient man from another planet...In fact...I have to think carefully to sort out the things I've really done myself from the memories that have been only instilled."

The four listeners sat around the open-air dinner table with undivided attention fixed on his words, in a spell of concentration that could not be disturbed by the clatter of their Bolivian help clearing the table. Charlie Ryan drank from his cup and began a more intensive questionnaire: "Let me review this once more, Doctor. You call the 'sarcophagus' a memory transcriber, by which you mean that one person's memory can be stored inside, for thousands of years, and then projected into another person's brain to become a living part of *his* memory."

"That's exactly what has happened to me, Charlie. I now carry the memory of two lives. Actually, such machines were used on Aesiris for teaching, or perhaps still are. Think what a boon to education it would be if every enquiring student could directly experience the thoughts of the world's geniuses. Relativity theory could become second nature to everyone. The events of history could be relived through the eyes of people who experienced those events. Years of study could be reduced to weeks; one could achieve a master's degree in any discipline by his twentieth birthday."

"A lot would still depend on the student's ability to absorb," Ryan commented.

"That's true, as I'm only too painfully aware with my present heavy head. But – who knows? – perhaps chemicals could be developed that could speed one's learning ability. Maybe the Aesir used such chemicals."

Leslie said: "You're both forgetting an essential part of the story. The people on Aesiris were, or are, largely an engineered breed of people, and by engineered I mean genetically engineered. Obviously in a population selected for intelligence the effectiveness of such teaching machines would be heightened, and the Aesir evidently took pains to improve their breeding. Lucirin, we're told, was an embryo that went awry."

"That's a certainty, Miss..." Doctor Niemeyer's voice trailed. "I'm afraid in the excitement when I arrived I didn't pay much attention to introductions." The bushy ends of his moustache painted a thin smile.

"Jennings. And it's Mrs. Call me Leslie. Mark here is my husband." She indicated the youthful man sitting next to her.

Sidney interjected: "Leslie and Mark are philologists. Their interest in ancient languages makes them naturals for this kind of work."

"Thank you, Sidney," Leslie replied. "In fact, we've already run across something of interest. Doctor, in your sleep today you became agitated, at times with vocalizations, and we took the liberty of recording them. We hope you don't mind."

"Not at all! I'd be delighted to hear what I said."

Mark rose from the table and ran to the Jennings' tent, returning with a tape-recorder. "Most of the recordings are garbled and incoherent, but I've noted one that is audible." He rewound the tape and stopped at a selected location on the counter.

"*...tem horsula metek shettel. Quad tansid nanzin ta! Plat motid, ni plasaad....*" Doctor Niemeyer's voice could be heard saying. Mark stopped the machine and asked: "Doctor, do you understand this language?"

"Not a word. That's what is so amazing about the memory transcriber. As Lucirin I can understand and speak that ancient tongue, because it's the meaning of each occasion that I experience and remember. The words are not mine as Doctor Niemeyer."

"Try to think, Doctor," Leslie requested. "It would mean a great deal to us if we could get a lead on a few words."

"Well, vaguely, I seem to associate it with the first meeting of Lucirin with Shura, just after the net was thrown over him. Yes...that's right. It's Lucirin's words telling Shura he had a full survival pack to prove he was a recent arrival on Gahes, and his disgust at Shura for stealing the pack. A literal word for word translation, though, is completely beyond me."

"What you've told us helps," Mark commented. "There's something else. You mentioned 'vul-canae' a few times in your sleep."

"Ah! That's an easy one. 'Vul-canae' literally means

'flight-ship'."

"That's interesting," Leslie said. "If I can go out on a limb with this one, 'vul-canae' sounds like 'volcano,' and 'canae,' if it corresponds to 'ship,' sounds like the Arawak word, 'canoe'. I don't know where the connection could be with 'volcano,' though."

"Perhaps in association with fire," Sidney guessed.

"That's it!" Mark exclaimed. "Were these 'vul-canae' rocket propelled, Doctor?"

"Not at all. Their propulsion was caused more by something like a surface tension, you know, like the movement of fine powder when you drop it into a bowl of still water. It seems that the surface tension was of space-time. As Lucirin I understand it, but not as Doctor Niemeyer. No, there must be another connection with fire."

"The annihilators," Ryan suggested, taking the group's attention. "It's not impossible. If ancient people heard the term 'vul-canae' and associated it with destructive heat rays, eventually the term could come to be applied to any severely destructive heat force. Perhaps the old Roman god, Vulcan, and 'volcano' were derived from 'vul-canae'."

A moment of silence was broken by Boyd: "If 'canae' means 'ship,' then 'vul' means 'flight'."

Leslie explained: "'Vul,' if it does mean 'flight,' would be a word not too far dissociated from modern languages. For instance, 'volar' in Spanish means 'to fly'."

The wild speculation became too much for Mark Jennings, who broke in with a questioning look at his wife: "What you and Charlie are suggesting, then, is a definite connection with Earth languages."

Ryan responded: "I'm certain that must be the case. Let's go to the beginning of this tale, when human prototypes were extracted for up-breeding. The description given of those times, of a cold planet with humanoids of brutish nature, sounds very much like the last Ice Age when large sections of Earth were glaciated. Since we know that Earth at that time was inhabited, because of numerous Neanderthal remains, the language of our spaceman may not only have been an Earth language, we may also be able to tie it into some of our modern tongues. Any language the Tsia spoke would undoubtedly have been so alien to primitive Earth brains and vocal organs that samples of human language, what existed at that time, would have had to be taken and retaught to their captive specimens, with the result that our spaceman spoke a remodelled human language."

Sydney Boyd listened quizzically, then confirmed: "So you're saying that Lucirin belonged to a race that was deliberately up bred by aliens from primitive humans of long ago!"

"That is what the doctor's story tells us, done for religious reasons. The aliens first established their new humans on Herez, then refined them even more for settlement on Aesiris, but left the more primitive type on Herez. That's why the difference between the two populations."

"With the difficulty that Aesiris had to be engineered for habitation," Doctor Niemeyer added. "Except for that, Aesiris was much like Earth at equatorial latitudes. In fact, come to think of it, that entire solar system seems like a scaled up version of our own if we think of Aesiris taking the place of Earth and Herez the place of Mars. The second sun in that binary system, Kolaster, would be a ringer for a larger Jupiter located farther from Kol than Jupiter from our Sun, and its planets like Gahes would be respective to the moons of Jupiter."

"And therefore a red sun, apparently less in size and mass than the main sun of that system," Ryan said. "That explains the black foliage of Gahes, because it would need to absorb all the radiation from the dim star, Kolaster.

"Let me place you on a more technical track now," he continued. "Yesterday we conjectured why the shell was made of copper, and I suggested the reason was the high electrical conductivity of that metal. A part of the doctor's account struck me while he was relating it: the copper helmet Lucirin wore when using his radiation device. It had the purpose of concealing him from some type of brain pattern identification probe. Could it be that the dome..."

"...is a similar device?" Boyd finished. "Sure! The 'sarcophagus' contains Lucirin's memory, and might be found by those probes if it weren't protected by a shield! Good thinking, Charlie!"

"It ties in with my fire theory about flight-ships too: conflict! Lucirin, when he came to Earth, was hiding from someone and didn't want them to discover his memory transcriber."

Leslie queried: "He also mentioned something at the beginning about Earth being threatened. What could that be about?"

"No doubt the conflict and danger are related," Ryan speculated. "We won't know until the 'sarcophagus' is used again."

"That won't be tonight," Doctor Niemeyer was quick to add. "My still weary brain needs a good night's rest, and possibly even a few days of relaxation before tackling the 'sarcophagus' again."

"A few days?" Mark asked.

Charlie Ryan rose from the table and slowly approached Doctor Niemeyer. "Doctor," he said, taking the pipe from his mouth, "we couldn't help noticing the strain this experience has been on you, and we wondered if you would mind a younger man taking your place in the dome. Sidney has volunteered, if you don't object."

The doctor was hesitant. "I hope you don't think ill of me," he finally said. "It would be wonderful if you could all use the machine, but you realize this project has meant a great deal to me for many years. Now it's payback time. But selfishness isn't my only reason for rejecting your offer, and I know it was made with the best intentions. We have to consider that I am the only trained archaeologist in our group, and there could be hints and insinuations in the dream of important connections to our present world. I'm probably the only person here who would perceive them. It doesn't hit me right away, of course, what those connections might be, but in weeks from now, as I reflect on this experience, those thoughts might come. And I'll be writing about this experience as well, so I'm going to need every scrap of information I can possibly squeeze out of it. Your point is well taken, though, and I'm not oblivious to the danger. That's why I'm going to relax for a few days and do some hiking. That ought to renew some of my energy."

Late evening returned to the small camp of enthusiasts. The doctor retired early, sleeping through a dream-packed night, with Leslie and Mark Jennings again taping his mutterings. The same occurred the next night after the doctor returned from his wandering in the desert.

Finally he was ready to again use the 'sarcophagus'. He entered the porthole and gazed upon the central box. Looking upon the curious crystal structure, the sensation of presence was still there; the crystal was already in communication with his mind. The sensation was now weaker, however, and the radiance of the interior was not as bright as he remembered. *Was the machine losing energy with usage?* he wondered.

Boyd, Ryan and Leslie Jennings peered from above through the dome's opening; Mark Jennings had left with the jeep to fetch a medic from Corque, the nearest town. The frail man placed the tiara on his head and took his position on the memory transcriber. The now familiar pattern of swirling cloud embraced him, and he felt himself sinking once more...into the world of Lucirin....

11

HERAS

STREAKS OF SNOW spread from my fur boots as I tread across the great white plain. Chill air nips my flesh. Kol hangs like a cold gem behind a cloud-enshrouded sky, casting faint shadows along the planet's wintry surface. Heras: a dismal world of bleak, empty landscapes.

"There, Captain," says Ologa, "just on the horizon you can see Quareg."

"Ah yes! To visit a city is a novel experience for me." With my comment Ologa shifts the parcel she carries, as if in substitution for a remark. "Isn't your burden getting heavy? We've been trekking a full day yet you haven't relieved yourself of its weight for an instant. Allow me to carry it to give you some rest."

Ologa shakes her head. "With respect, Sire, I prefer to carry it myself. It is I who our Master charged with its keeping, and if misfortune yet befalls us I wouldn't trust the resolve of one outside Balam. Besides, the worst of our journey is through since we reached the plain of Quareg. But we can't delay. Second sun is already low, and if we find ourselves without shelter come nightfall, these goat-skin hides will protect us little against the biting winter winds."

At evening we are within the confines of the city, and already Ologa's warning proves true, as streams of fine snow streak above the roofs of the buildings and cut into my face when I pass out of the narrow alleys. People of the city are returning to their dwellings, some walking, some riding ox-carts, and occasionally the scene is contrasted by an Aesir or high ranking Herasian using a levitator.

"The crowded streets are to our advantage. They make us less noticeable," Ologa assures.

"I've never seen such congestion." I must shout my words to be heard in the biting wind. "These people, all clothed in animal skins, and of such variety: thin, fat, short, and tall. And the buildings! Are there no fine houses in all Quareg?"

"For sure, there is...one." Likewise with raised voice, close to my ear, Ologa points to an imposing structure barely visible in the waning light, and says: "There you'll find the comfort and wealth of Aesiris, from which Herasians are deprived. That's the Capitol, where Aesir rulers reside with their treasonous Herasian puppets.

"Hurry, Lucirin, don't slow your pace. Soon the crowds will clear and we'll be alone on the city's streets, that will make us prey for questions."

Again I lower my eyes to not trip over the roughly hewn stones of the street. Dry swirls of snow wisp over the hard surfaces. Soon the crowds disappear, and cold darkness is upon us except for the light of hearth fires squeezing out between wooden planks of doors and shutters. After numerous turns, Ologa stops before one of the houses and pounds on its timber door. The wait is tense, which I use to observe the dwelling. It is one typical of Quareg: low and plain, built of stone, mud and wood with large beams of lumber framing its doorway. The heavy door is jarred open and in the warm rays of light from behind an old, bearded head appears. "Who's there?" it demands.

"It's Ologa, and I bring a friend."

"I know of no Ologa."

"I bear a gift. Can we discuss it inside?"

The old man hesitates, then opens the door for us to enter. We step into the dwelling and immediately upon the door being closed Ologa performs her complicated hand ritual, the same that I first saw on Degras. The old man says, to my astonishment: "We be expecting you." A woman and a girl appear, and the atmosphere becomes relaxed.

"I'm going to have to learn that."

"You must be Lucirin, rebel Aesir who escaped Gahes. I calls myself Eloez. The signal you saw we share only in Balam, and has more to it than meets the outsider's eye. You're a valuable man, Lucirin, outsider yet, for your work in Heimbal's service. Both of you please accept welcome to my humble home. My family prepares the evening meal, which, for sure after your long walk, you'll partake with us."

Ologa is quick to accept: "A good Herasian meal gives renewed strength and warms the innards."

Eloez's wife requests from the joining room: "Come in and seat yourselves by the hearth, friends. Supper will take not long."

The evening meal passes simply and quietly, and when finished, Eloez, Ologa and I enter the living chamber to discuss events. Ologa and I seat ourselves in two old, but not uncomfortable, chairs, while Eloez, with a slight, deep throated complaint, throws a slab of manure into the fire-place. He turns, still bent over, his rough, brown cassock hanging loosely in front of his belly except where it is pulled up by his waist-cord, and collapses into a well upholstered chair next to Ologa. "I trust your ship had no trouble when it entered Herasian domain," he grunts.

"None whatever. That was a surprise since I had visions of alerting the entire Aesir fleet. As it happened, we slipped to

the surface only a day's walk from Quareg. I don't think we were spotted once. Such callousness is difficult to understand, knowing Aesir prudence."

"It would be no surprise, my friend, if you knew the lay on Heras. It was by scheme, not accident, that you set foot on this soil."

Both Herasians turn their gaze toward me with looks of satisfaction, even a tint of arrogance. The blank expression on my own face solicits Ologa to explain: "Eloez means, Lucirin, that there be for a long time secret talk between Heras and Degras. From that Eloez knew we were coming. Every officer in Balam by now knows we're here. When we entered Herasian domain they made the sighters blind for a while."

My voice cannot hide its note of delight: "In that case I've grossly underestimated your organization. In order to affect the defence of this planet your members must have worked their way into very sensitive positions." A strange mixture of cultures is evidently taking place on Heras, at least among the Balam leadership. Looking at this very provincial man, Eloez, I would never suspect that he was in any way knowledgeable of the superluminal devices used by Heimbal for telepathic transmission. Possibly I credit him too much, for any instruction can be taught without genuinely understanding its operation.

"Of course, we deliberately made it our business for Aesir not to reckon us proper," the old man says. "Soon, very soon, we can remove that deception."

"Soon?"

"Soon," Eloez repeats, giving a slight nodding motion to his head. "I'll give you a brief story of what happened on our world since the last days of Heimbal here: When Aesir returned their control many ages ago, the Balam disciples went under cover. It was obvious to Aesir, likes it was to everyone else, that the teachings of our greatest leader were not fully scoured, but the Aesir were sure that with time, over ages, our old beliefs would die. Such opinion only revealed the ignorance of Aesir towards Balam, for we knew that our Master escaped and was safe, and as long as he lives our faith lives too."

The fervour in the old man's voice convinces me I should never reveal the true nature of Heimbal as I found it on Degras. A simple people could never accept a console of circuitry as equivalent to a human being, let alone a man-deity, and any attempt on my part toward enlightenment would bring unnecessary distrust, if not extra danger, on my head. No, it is best to let them revel in their primitive spiritualism.

Eloez continues: "Over the ages our league strengthened, always under cover, always unseen. When a youth reveals displeasure with government, he or she is sent into a cloister of Balam, of which there be many, all separate and secret from one another and from society at large. I'm a vicar in one cloister for twenty-two years. We grow not just in number, but in strength beyond our numbers. You came here in a stolen starcruiser, without discover, and that be a small show of how we followers of Balam wormed our way, unknown, into the channels of power. One important step remains, that when finished will return the glory of Heras."

"I hope to be of assistance in furthering your rebellion. The sooner Heras shakes off its Veradi overlords the sooner I'll be a completely free man. What's left to do?"

"Over the ages, piece by piece, deep underground in our hidden caves, we build an altar to our great patron, by his secret plan. When we finish that altar Heimbal will once more belong to us. That altar today nears finish."

The old man's eyes become transfixed in a rigid forward stare, straight into my own. Fanaticism is in his face, mellowed but slightly with time. His mouth is firm under strings of long, white hair that hang limply to his shoulders. His arms are held stiffly out to grasp the rests of his seat, in a grip that turns his wrinkled knuckles white.

The moment of mystic silence is broken by Ologa: "Friends, let's not forget the gift I brought from the Illustrious One. It's likely another piece for the altar, that brings us closer to our day of justice."

Throughout the evening Ologa has been sitting with her parcel from Degras close at hand. Perhaps now, finally, I'll learn what it contains.

"Yes, Ologa," Eloez replies, his head turning slowly towards her and the former iron look in his eyes becoming misty. "It is time."

Ologa gently places the shoulder bag on the floor in front of her feet, opens the cords that hold the bag shut, and from the inside withdraws a cylindrical container with a number of mechanisms around its base, one of which looks very much like a respirator. Knowing that Heimbal today is nothing more than an ingenious machine, I dismiss this possibility.

"The gift lays inside the cylinder," Eloez says, but Ologa is puzzled in removing what is obviously a protective shroud.

"Let me help," I volunteer, and placing my fingers on its molecular disengagement rings, the cylinder separates from its base. Left sitting on the base, revealed in the shimmering light of the hearth-fire, is a silver sphere, a little more than the size of a human head.

"Ologa!" Eloez gasps, crouching on his knees with his arms apart as if to embrace the object, "You know what you brought?"

"No Sire! I know only from where it is fetched. None other than the great Heimbal instructed me how..."

"This is the most sacred possession of all Balam: the cabes-trebla!"

Eloez's excited voice brings his wife and daughter scurrying into the living room, to gaze in amazement at the gift brought from Degras. For myself, Ologa's unfinished comment sets me thinking that I too have seen this silver sphere, as the experience awakens my recollection of Heimbal and the sophisticated machine I found in his underground hide-out. In the center of that machine sat a silver sphere, exactly the same as the one now before us, if it is not that very one. The memory is revealing, for the so-called altar of these backward Herasians suddenly makes sense: it is none other than a similar device built here on this planet. And this 'cabes-trebla' is the master circuitry, carried from Degras by Ologa to be installed in the new machine. *Once that installation is complete Heimbal will certainly live again on Heras.*

"We waste not an instant," Eloez says as he awkwardly rises to his feet. "Ologa, I'll give you names of seven others. You bring them here tonight. Put on my heavy cape for protection against the night winds, and bring them to this house. This is important, for sure."

A flurry of activity seizes Eloez's family; his wife scurries off and returns with a heavy woollen cape, the typical Herasian garment I saw popular in the streets. Eloez places something into Ologa's hand with a warning to beware of questioning strangers. Ologa flings the cape around herself, ties the inside cords, and is gone. Eloez returns to the living room.

I ask: "What is so important about the cabes-trebla that cannot wait until morning?"

Eloez wrings his hands anxiously, his face wearing a furrowed brow: "Friend Lucirin, there's a gathering of Aesir force at Quareg. Eight or nine vul-canae land every day, from all over Kolaria, and many are of a heavy class, like your star-cruiser. We of Balam never pierced the highest ruling circles, those are Aesir, but we think the reason is a final scathe to rid Heras of Balam for all time. You see, the Aesir know of our business on Heras. Until this evening I had no idea why that thrust be now, at the present day, but with the cabes-trebla that reason is clear."

I make a guess: "The Aesir have discovered that Heimbal is no longer on Degras."

Eloez's white eyebrows rise. "Yes...for sure, that's correct." There is a pause before he resumes speaking, sensing I have already estimated the importance of the silver sphere. "The cabes-trebla, as I say, is the most sacred possession of all Balam. It's the last magical piece for our altar, that once again will allow Heimbal life among his people. We need to complete that altar before the Aesir begin their inquisition, if that be their purpose, and for the seven initiates in the magical rites of construction I sent Ologa tonight. In less than five days Heimbal will again walk among us."

"Tell me, Eloez, was it not rather, er...reckless of Heimbal to entrust so sacred an object as the cabes-trebla to fugitives like myself and Ologa, especially when he must have known it would initiate this kind of response?"

"The Aesir have some change since you were last on their world. You're already familiar with their aura-scanner, that reveals a person's drift to their Belief?"

"I am. It was their aura-scanner that cinched my banishment to Gahes."

"Yes," Eloez affirms knowledgeably. "Well, now a further change of that aura-scanner sees not only how Belief-bent a subject is, but also sees his drift towards Balam, and if he be already a member. We fear they'll use the scanner to screen the whole litter of Heras, and banish all of Balam to Gahes. For sure that would mean the death of our rebellion, and of our faith. For that reason Heimbal was forced, by luck at a time when the altar nears finish."

"I see, and when do you think the Aesir will begin this total screening process? Surely it is an undertaking that will raise some concern in the general populace."

"That knowledge we lack, indeed, as I say, we have no sure savvy if an inquisition be the Veradi plan. A possibility presents itself, thought. In three nights a social frolic will take place in the Capitol, and there for sure there'll be free knowledge afloat. If we could infiltrate that frolic..."

"Think no more of it. I'll do it. It will be an excellent opportunity for me to get a close look at the enemy I face on Heras."

"What? You? Oh no!" Eloez shakes his head. "For you it's too risky."

"Not at all. A meeting like that is a natural setting for an Aesir accent. I've changed in appearance since leaving Aesiris, so if anyone is there whom I have met before, I'm doubtful if I would be recognized. I have a well-armed ship at my disposal if anything goes wrong, and supplies of the appropriate wear from the ship's wardrobe. About all that is missing is some false identification."

Eloez muses over the proposal. "You make a strong point. Identification is the toughest. It's by brain sign, the same as on Aesiris. We have records of people safe to use, if you could alter yours to suit."

"Leave those technicalities to me. Just give me the word."

"I agree," he says finally. "The mission is yours. Take care. And take one of your Herasian maids who can warn you on Herasian etiquette. I'll look through our identification files for the two of you."

I spend that night in the attic of Eloez's rustic house. Outside, the wind rages unceasingly, but the rigors of the day allow sleep to come easily, even in these strange quarters. I am disturbed only once when I hear voices from the room below, evidently of the seven people initiated in the 'magical rites' to install the cabes-trebla. They soon disappear again into the howling night. With morning I have a hearty breakfast, receive two brain pattern identification tablets from Eloez for falsifying identification, and begin the lone trek back to my ship and companions.

12

THE PARTY

"This whole idea is insane! Imagine us, the two biggest outcasts in all Kolaria: spies! Right under the noses of every ruling family!" Arrana has been in a disgruntled mood since I told her of my espionage plan. "I'm a fool to go along like this!"

"Have a little confidence in technology. As long as we keep Eloez's circuitry intact we shouldn't have difficulty." A dresser's arms spiral rapidly to finish my leg dressing. "I haven't survived by lying back and letting events pass over me. We're the best people for the job. Remember, our freedom, even our lives, depends on success of the Herasian revolt."

"Oh! I know," she admits. "Still, I feel uneasy."

"ENTERING LANDING STATION."

"There! What better evidence could we have that events are under control? We're landing our ship right in the Capitol flight port, thanks to our Balam friends falsifying reports."

"But I feel out of place. I've never worn a gown like this before. How can I pass for a high lady?" Both Arrana and I are dressed for the occasion, she in the long gown of the highest female peerage and I in an Aesir ceremonial tunic.

"You look beautiful. I've no doubt Herasian gentlemen will be giving you their attention. Just remember, you are Dame Siebal and I am Captain Naiad. But you needn't worry about the guests. The greatest danger will come when we pass the identification scope."

"This Siebal and Naiad...We're taking the places of the

dead?"

"We are. Eloez explained it on the morning I left his house. Herasian gentry have their brain patterns read when hospitalized and nursed by medics in the Balam underground. If they die, conspirators working in the census bureau make sure their records aren't removed from the census computer, so their identification can be reused on spy missions. Heimbal hasn't let one trick escape him. That should give us comfort to be on the side of the conspirators."

My assurances do little to placate Arrana. In a levitator as we pass over the flight port to the Capitol building she again comments in a voice that cannot hide her concern: "So many vul-canae, Lucirin. If fortune turns against us we'll stand no chance at all."

"You worry too much. Not one of those ships you see is on standby alert. On the other hand, what a prize when we leave the Capitol: we could destroy most of their fleet."

"You can't be serious!"

"Of course I'm serious. It's utter madness to concentrate ships in one port like this. It shows how much the Aesir underestimate Balam, and justifiably so. It was our meeting with Heimbal that tipped fate in his favor, and he wasn't slow to take advantage of us."

Red and blue lights puncture the darkness below, displaying shifting streams of wind tossed snow in their luminance. Not far in the distance lies the mammoth cruiser of a Veradi. "Yes, Arrana..." I turn to look through our levitator canopy at the number and variety of ships, "...we're likely to see high ranking officials here tonight."

The circular portal of the Capitol engulfs us as we enter the bright interior of that building. We exit our vehicle, Arrana straightens her gown, and we proceed to walk, casually, down a long corridor, past groups of smiling guests engaged in pleasant conversation, to an immense, sunken arena occupying the heart of this magnificent edifice. We dawdle momentarily at the head of a broad, stone staircase to absorb the splendour of the spectacle. The great building stretches overhead, displaying decorations of stone lace-work, crystal lattice, holographic reliefs picturing idealized scenes on Heras, and mathematical patterns. A multitude of people is gathered in the arena below, comprised mostly of the propertied Herasian gentry dancing to an imported Aesir melody. More people are seated to the sides, in alcoves leading off from the arena, and on the corridor level, all dressed in the finest raiment and ornamental stones. The Aesir, by contrast, remain dressed in their comparatively simple tunics, their austere figures clearly discernable in the crowd. My temporary deprivation of such cultural refinement has made me no less susceptible to its seductiveness, the scene giving mixed sentiments of belonging with those of rejection owing to my forced expulsion from that favored elite.

Arrana, too, is visibly awed by the prodigious soiree. "I never imagined anything like this," she murmurs, then clutches my arm and asks close to my ear: "When does it happen?"

"When does what happen?"

"Don't play stupid. The identification probe!"

"We've already passed it," I chuckle. "You underestimate my technical talent."

"Already?" she asks, her eyebrows raised.

"Sure! It was in a small room off the corridor as we passed. Submission to a visible identification test would be humiliating to dignitaries like these. Now relax, and act your part. Let's see what information we can glean from the party."

We take each step down to the arena leisurely, smiling to the unfamiliar faces that pass on the staircase. By the time we reach the arena floor the strains of music have stopped, the melodious sounds replaced by discordant chatter as the guests regroup themselves into numerous cliques throughout the floor, some laughing, some flirting, and others engaged in serious conversation. It is the latter which we judge most beneficial to our mission, and we quietly steer a course toward one group of well-tailored Herasians pressing an opinion on an Aesir.

"Umph!" Arrana, it seems, has already attracted the eye of Herasian men. A big fellow not watching where he's going, or on the pretence of not doing so, swings around and stumbles into her, who being the lighter is thrown off balance and is visibly disturbed by the joust.

"I beg the pardon of the beautiful mistress!" he says. "Please forgive this clumsy oaf," then laughingly, "With a frame like mine manoeuvring on the social floor be a task best suited to the most gifted diplomacy."

The Herasian is certainly a large man, with a great mound of fat on his belly that moves up and down in short spasms with his nasal laughter. He places his hands at his sides as if to display his bulk more fully, and leans back to observe us through beady eyes set in a puffed, good-humored face.

"Your apology is completely accepted," Arrana says politely and wishes to move off since it is not our intention to become intimate with any of the guests.

"They calls me Babu. It's a name my friends gave me because I talk so much. Never know when to quit once I start." He wheezes a silent, jerky laugh. "I'm a merchant, trading is my passion. I trade all over Kolaria in everything you can imagine, from the finest cloth to the finest foods fit for a gourmet's palate. Would you believe I even have an item from Gahes? Now there's a planet I see not often, and with the greatest reluctance."

I comment: "With all your trading and wealth you must

have a strong interest in preserving stability on Heras."

"For sure. The trade commissioner is a friend, better I say he's a relative, but keep that behind your ear," he mentions with a flurry of his chubby fingers. "I don't usually divulge such privity. Ah yes, you'll not find a more loyal subject than this Babu; but I say, I haven't seen you before." Looking at me, "Are you new to the ranks?"

"Not entirely. I patrol the Fringe. My station is on Kirigna and there's not much chance of fraternizing from that distance."

"Too bad! Too bad! Kirigna, ah yes, I be there once or twice. Not much there at the edge of Kolaria. I say, this emergency, it's pulling you military people from far and wide. You think it'll take long?"

"...The emergency...?"

"Well...whatever it is you people come here for. I'll be happy when it's over."

Shrugging my shoulders, "A few days."

"Fine! A few days be tolerable. Still, I think I'll take a holiday, or strike some business on Dabinor. Heras could be messy for a while and I do detest violence." Babu momentarily becomes contemplative, then his bulbous mouth again breaks into a meaty grin: "Oh! There's an Aesir friend, Captain Pelin...Oh Captain...over here...come and meet two new acquaintances, Captain...uh, sorry, I don't know your names..."

"Naiad," I respond, "and my companion is Dame Siebal."

Curse this Babu! I had hoped to make my presence as little felt as possible by simply listening to conversations and asking a polite question or two; now I am face to face with a fellow Aesir who will be curious about my activities with the fleet.

Pelin greets us with a pleasant smile. "Are you stationed on Heras or just here for the emergency?" he asks.

"Just the emergency."

"Ah yes! Captain Naiad is stationed at Kirigna. To call flight-ships from so far shows the worth the Rasan places on this tiny, backward planet, don't you think, Pelin?"

Pelin's smile fades. "Yes," he says slowly, "but it was my understanding that flight-ships at the Fringe were on the look-out for aliens."

Aliens! Can the Aesir already be aware of Heimbal's two dead giant companions? If so, Pelin has revealed information that may be of importance. I venture a guess: "You mean the giants? Yes, that's true, however the Command has judged that danger not as severe as the danger Balam now presents to Heras, and has released a few ships from the Fringe. I was lucky."

My answer appears to satisfy him. His lack of puzzlement could mean he knows about giants as well as aliens. I press further: "Owing to the distance involved I've just today arrived at the Capitol and I probably missed some important meetings. Perhaps you could bring me up to date on recent developments."

"I see. Then you didn't attend the viceroy's lecture this morning. Is that right?"

"That's correct."

Arrana, while remaining cordial to the intimate chatter Babu has begun with her, keeps an ear on Pelin and has become more tense with our meeting this Aesir. She distinctly does not like such questioning and what she considers my reckless lying. Behind me the strains of the orchestra begin playing again, and with the cue guests move off or onto the large floor depending on their disposition for entertainment or discussing events. Pelin beckons us to move to the side, which we do through streams of laughing people headed for the floor.

"Our discussion with the viceroy this morning was most important." Pelin raises his voice to be heard above the background din. "I guess every commander except you was present, but I can supply you with the main points, if you wish."

"Now there's a cordial chap for you, Naiad," Babu motions to me. "Pelin is the kind of Aesir I get along with best; he's not rigid like some others I know. I say, you're lucky we met!" then, with a wink towards Arrana, adds: "although our meeting was a little hard on your charming Siebal." His enormous stomach bounces in short chuckles.

I request from Pelin: "Yes, I would be grateful if you would fill me in on whatever I missed this morning," indeed reflecting on our good fortune to receive a cache of information from so willing a source.

Pelin places his hands behind his back and leans slightly forward in a stance characteristic of Aesir, and begins: "The cult of Balam has been increasing its activities on Heras in the past years, which has convinced the Veradi that something must be done to eradicate it in a once-and-for-all effort. The result has been further research into psycho-physiological changes in the electro-neurological systems of animal life forms, with emphasis, of course, on the human-animal life form. A device has been perfected where it is now possible to detect a member, or a potential member, of the Balam cult, and we may have a demonstration of that invention later tonight."

I can see in Arrana's eyes that she is making a mental note not to be present for that demonstration, and I entirely sympathize with her sentiment.

"It has become possible to test every Herasian for his or her empathy with that horrendous cult, and the original intention of the Veradi was to do that slowly, after a general program of ultrasonic, subliminal persuasion in the main population centers of Quareg and Tasis. Such a propaganda campaign would be necessary to reduce resistance, possibly even violence, against the project. Naturally that would take time, and it now appears we do not have that time. The Veradi fear that a mind duplication of Heimbal, the cult's founder, has been constructed on Heras and are taking no chances. They're now going to initiate the detection program without the mass ultrasonic persuasion preliminaries."

"That's the reason for collecting a fleet at Quareg: in case violence should erupt."

"Yes. Herasians already consider Aesir rule an imposition, and the intimate testing may be provoking. The main purpose of the fleet is preventative; to make resistance appear so hopeless it will be discouraged before it begins. There isn't much likelihood our weapons will be used against the Herasian rabble."

"Did the viceroy mention when the program would begin?"

"We'll begin with the first suspects tomorrow. Those who fail the test will be off to Gahes not long thereafter."

That is certainly information Eloez would appreciate. A general directive must be issued this very night for the leaders of Balam to go into immediate hiding. With Pelin's last words I can feel Arrana's stare, pressing me with her own directive: *leave the Capitol!* I am inclined to agree since we have confirmed Eloez's fears that a purge is imminent, and the sooner we leave the more time will be allowed for the Balam leaders to seek refuge.

The music from the floor subsides and in its place the voice of an Aesir makes an announcement: "Distinguished guests: as is the custom during our gatherings we intermix business with the festivities. Now we have to deprive you of all Aesir flight-captains. A meeting for them to attend will shortly be held in the green alcove at the north end of the hall. It will concern our finding on Gahes the remains of a flight-ship crew that had been stationed at Degras. That is all."

Arrana and I look at each other; the taut lines of her face, that were provoked by my seemingly careless approach to this whole gathering, have given way to lines of fear.

"What's the matter with you two?" Pelin asks. "Aren't you coming to the meeting, Naiad? It's mandatory, you know."

"I'll be with you in a moment," then to Babu: "I have a word to say to Dame Seibal, alone, if you don't mind."

Arrana and I step a few paces away, into the loneliness of the crowd. She grasps my hand and whispers: "We must leave, *now,* before it's too late!"

"And how would that look? It's not as serious as it seems. They know nothing about us, only that 0-7-1's crew met death on Gahes. Besides, I'm curious to know what will be discussed." Her eyes roll up in exasperation. "Babu will be your escort while I attend the meeting."

"Delightful!" she snarls.

In the alcove, a crowd of Aesir captains circles a viewing area where a commander is standing ready to present the findings. He begins: "As mentioned in the announcement, we have located the crew of flight-ship 0-7-1, killed in a primitive attack by a band of Gahean criminals. I have here a sample of the weapons used." He presents an arrow used by the Arransin in their raid. "Fortunately we have an account of the attack made possible by memory projection from several of the deceased crew. A transport happened upon the scene shortly after the disaster..."

Memory projections from the dead brains of Arrana's victims! My heart palpitates at the thought of this whole company of Aesir captains witnessing Arrana and her followers at their deadly chore. Not annihilating the enemy cadavers was a slip-up!

"...We're most fortunate in having located our comrades' remains, but several factors helped: the event took place close to the wreck of a research vessel that the transport and also, we believe, the star cruiser, had been looking for, on a narrow projection of land into the sea, exposing the cadavers. The raiders also blasted a nearby hill with annihilator, for reasons we don't know."

"A question, Commander," one of the captains requests. "It's inconceivable to me, as I'm sure it is to many others here, that a primitive band of criminals could overtake the crew of an Aesir star-cruiser, then use the cruiser to escape. How could that happen, and where would they obtain technical instructions to use that ship?"

"A most pertinent question, Captain. Let's not forget, it's not only ignorant Herasians that are banished to Gahes. The planet serves as a repository for the worst of all Kolaria, including Aesiris. We suspect a technical genius by the designation Lucirin, twenty-nine Andra-naudae, to be behind this disaster, since he can no longer be detected on Gahes by cephalo-probe. We'll give details on this criminal after the account of the attack."

The Commander motions for the projection to begin and leaves the circular viewing area. Moments later the first images appear: the last sights of one of 0-7-1's former crewmembers. The projection starts where the ship's portal is already opened and the crewmember hurries out to the beach. Maiori is clearly seen, bound and gagged in front of the immobilized warriors outside the time field. Most noticeable is Arrana, poised with her bow ready to strike. It's only a question of moments, from this visual and others perhaps even better defined, before she is recognized by Pelin. If he is still uncertain, there will be a visual of me from Aesiris. He will certainly put the two together.

I had stationed myself near the entrance of the alcove as a precaution, and take my leave from that dim interior. Arrana is quick to notice my re-entering the open floor and runs over to meet me. "Let's go!" I tell her, "but not so fast we'll attract attention."

That effort is futile since the guests are already looking in our direction, wondering why a vul-canae captain is not attending a compulsory meeting, a situation not helped by the bloated figure of Babu waddling to catch up. "Wait!" he shouts in his caked voice. "We still have much to discuss. The frolic isn't half over and I do enjoy your company."

We reach the foot of the stairs when it happens: the Aesir captains storm out of the alcove, led by Pelin who stops to give a scouting glance around the immense hall. There's no time to lose, we must run, except Babu has succeeded in attaching himself to Arrana's arm in a firm effort at congeniality. "I hope I haven't offended you in any waaaagg...."

Babu's voice trails in gargled blood with the swish of iron in Arrana's hand. The life fluid streams from his mouth as the writhing mountain of flesh collapses to the floor. Screams from the guests pierce the air. We leap up the stairs and down the entrance corridor, only to see Palatine guards rushing toward us.

I yank Arrana into the ill concealed room off the corridor containing the identification probe. "Latch off me!" she warns. "Now what? We have guards closing on us from both ends! Why didn't we leave when we had a chance?"

The communicator feels cold, pressed between my eyes: "0-7-1, come immediately, one annihilator through portal, low power, wait at portal."

Anxious moments pass as the footsteps of our pursuers

come closer, then halt at the door. There's much shouting. We squeeze flat on the floor, mouths open and arms over our heads in anticipation of our ship's deadly blast. Suddenly, a flash with the deafening roar of a vul-canae annihilator streaks down the corridor. A guard is flung into our probe chamber, flattening on its opposing wall. Clouds of dust from blasted rock and steam from evaporated protoplasm fill the hot corridor as we stumble to the building portal, where our flight-ship is waiting. Neither of us can speak, being stunned and deafened by the blast, our throats clogged by the noxious fumes.

"Hurry!" a voice commands through the cloud of smoke and dust. "There come others!"

Members of our crew aid us onto 0-7-1's landing ramp, then station themselves by the portal to fire annihilators into the Capitol. Glancing back, I see flames at the end of the once or-nate corridor, now charred and filled with smoke.

"0-7-1, immediate attack pattern five over flight port, low intensity charge, power four!"

"COMMAND RECEIVED, AM EXECUTING."

Arrana holds her hand to the base of her throat, leans against a bulkhead and gasps the clean air. "What madness have you in store for us next?" she demands.

"Come to the viewer and find out."

The bursts of fire on the viewing table show our engagement on the multitude of sleeping ships. "We're attacking the full fleet?" she exclaims. "We should be fleeing, Lucirin, as fast as we can!"

"Not yet. The ships below are asleep. We can use these moments very profitably by teaching the Aesir the folly of un-preparedness." Turning my attention to the fighters collected around the viewer: "Arransin! A night of vengeance!"

A screaming yell issues from the band. My companions

are delighted by the display of explosive power they see on the viewer, as 0-7-1 continues its deadly course over the flight port. One ship after another bursts into star-like explosions, the brightness magnified by the snow of the port. Shortly the whole area is speckled with red, yellow, green and blue embers of burning ships that lend magnificence to the winter night.

The spectacle, however, is far from overwhelming the wily Arrana: "From what I know of this ship, my dear Captain, we possess more destruction power than you're unleashing on those Aesir vessels."

"A most astute observation. The Herasian revolt must soon occur after tonight, and crippled ships still in the flight port will be captured. They'll be repairable and usable in our own fleet against Aesiris if not too badly damaged." Speaking to 0-7-1: "Cease attack. Take flight path to Tarusal Sector, maximum speed."

"RECEICED, AN EXECUTING."

The scene on the viewer gradually changes. Heras becomes a shrinking globe as we race into the far corners of Kolaria.

"VUL-CANAE LEAVING HERAS."

The magnified table reveals star-cruisers following our trajectory: twelve, eighteen, the number keeps growing. An unusual silence pervades the command section. There's a change from enthusiasm to uneasiness among my crew. "Have no concern," I tell them, "0-7-1 can outrun anything in the galaxy." Turning next to the communicator, I send a message to Eloez, warning him of the Aesir plan. "That ought to give extra incentive to the revolt."

A Herasian day passes, then another, and still no word of the revolt. The Arransin grow edgy as the silent chase continues. For three days the Aesir remain in pursuit but have made no significant gain. Finally at the end of the third day the squadron breaks its chase formation. Cheering erupts amongst the crew.

"Quiet!" I urge them. "Heimbal is going to address us."

From the ship's speakers the deep voice of Heimbal is heard throughout: "Faithful friends of Balam, our Revolt is won. A new regime is born on Heras. Since you played a grand part in our victory, because you maimed many of the hated Aesir ships and lured many others away at great risk, and distracted the rulers from the soon revolt of Herasians, more the service you did in delivering the cabes-trebla, you'll receive special honours in our new regime, in particular Captain Lucirin. I appoint him Minister of Defence. Heras waits your return."

Yells of exuberance break from my Arransin crew with the end of the message. We join in the laughter of self-congratulation, and once again I find myself the object of adulation, of every member except one. Standing off from the group in a quiet pose, taking no part in the revelry yet observing me with her placid eyes and thin smile, that suggest mixed feelings of despair yet admiration, is Maiori.

13

CAMPORA

A VEIL OF LAZY smoke floats from the flight port into the clear
Herasian sky, days after our pummelling the fleet of sleeping
ships. Arrana and I stand in the middle of the port with her
unruly band, looking over the field of destruction.

She gibes: "So, my dear Captain, you're going to restore
these ships before the Aesir return." As usual, she's sceptical.

"It's a gamble we'll have to take, isn't it?" I assess the magnitude of the task. Light class ships are completely gutted, their
blackened parts spewed onto peppered snow. Heavier ships are
still intact.

"A gamble we're sure to loose. 0-7-1 did its job too well."

"Maybe. Right now I would say your prediction of failure is
premature. Heimbal is presently negotiating with the Aesir for
the right of access to Degras. Why he wants that I don't know,
but he's using prisoners as collateral. Some of them are Veradi,
and while we have them the Aesir will not attack. We'll have
time to make repairs. But I can't do it all myself. I'll have to
train you and your followers on what to do. I'll supervise. We'll
concentrate on the most powerful ships first."

Night and day we work. The Herasians move throughout the

half ruined ships, tearing out baked circuits, exploded mani-folds, broken indicators and fused leads, each which has to be repaired or replaced from cannibalised parts. One day on a visit to Arrana to give her help, she peers down from a trajector bay. "Lucirin, you look tired," she sympathizes, still holding her hands above her head in the bowls of the ship. Discarded parts form a disarrayed pile on the flight port floor at the base of her ladder. Her face is smeared with dirt.

"I *am* tired. Your Herasian kinsmen have to be instructed on the most basic elements of flight-ship construction. It's been ages since I've had a full ration of sleep."

"Did you expect different? If they know nothing of Aesir technology, whose fault is that? Can you believe Herasians never wanted it, that we preferred to live like animals com-pared to Aesir?" She climbs down her ladder to confront me with her point.

"Relax, Arrana. I didn't mean it as a criticism. I guess we're both tired from all this haste. Actually, I'm delighted. The plan is going well. Your followers know what's at stake. They're motivated."

"Herasians are accustomed to hard work. This is a far dif-ferent world from Aesiris. We don't have everything done for us on command. Maybe that's why Aesir delays their return. They know they're in for a fight."

"Yes, their hesitancy shows what cowards they are, or rather the Veradi. But their delay has served us well."

"For sure it served you well. I see how the people treat you, like a hero."

Arran's remark is another confirmation of my old lesson on adversity and survival. Freedom from Aesir rule was slow to dawn on Herasians. At first they could not believe their suc-cess, but with time conviction became more certain and with it my own fame and popularity. That lesson has now placed a whole world at my disposal. I'll use that lesson yet again, and should it prove itself once more I'll at last have my vengeance upon the cowardly Veradi.

For a year we worked to restore the ruined fleet, and during this time a mystery unfolded on Heras with the reascendance of Heimbal to authority. In the streets, in the bazaars, in the theatres one hears the continuous campaign to win the loyalty of the population, utilizing the subliminal devices and persuasion techniques captured from the Aesir, in the service of Balam. Conversions have not been difficult, for Heimbal knows his people well. Herasians have shown considerable predilection for the new observances.

Once every thirty-eight days a grand festival is conducted on the floor of the Capitol, ordered by Heimbal as a religious obligation. People flock to the occasions that display none of the refinement of similar gatherings under the former ruling Herasians and Aesir. The motivation is simple and primitive, to release passions under an intense emotion field, and never could I have imagined the wild abandonment that overtakes Herasians attending these festivals. They expend more energy than over days of work, only in the end to collapse in stacks of depleted bodies, relying on friends and relatives, who did not attend the festival, for their return home. Herasians come in such numbers, from all over the planet, that many have to be refused entry into the Capitol; each festival brings lines of people to the Capitol gate, and often one sees the same faces time and again. And with each event it is usual to behold poor wretches who, not in time for the period's festival and finding themselves above the quota for entry, scratch and claw on the hard planks of the gate in a frenzy of grief. For Herasians the festivals have become an obsession, and I well understand now

how the legend of Heimbal has gripped them so profoundly.

When the orgy is at its highest pitch, the Grand Master appears and brings sudden silence to the sweating multitude. In the same repetitive tones the image commands: "Children of Balam, the moment of your fulfilment is at hand. Who among you is prepared?" - a request that brings a rush of guests, each waving his or her arms frantically in a foolish effort to attract attention from the apparition. "Let the choice be made," the image drones each time before fading, which brings priests of Balam amid the jubilant crowd to test the volunteers with aurascanners. That in itself is not surprising, knowing that an aurascanner has been perfected by the Aesir to test one's disposition to Balam; what *is* surprising is that every person selected by the solemn priests is led away from the crowd, *never to be seen again.*

After observing one such festival Maiori and I retire to my quarters to ponder the mystery. "I should loan you my maids," she scolds. "It looks like you could use them with all these scrolls, maps, diagrams and who knows what, scattered everywhere, even over the floor." She holds her hands apart in mock disgust. "I'm surprised that you should live in such Herasian squalor."

"I use my living quarters for work and study as much as for relaxation. I don't believe in the luxurious frivolousness common for Balam officials."

"I was just teasing. Actually, I like these quarters of yours, especially this oriel overlooking the Capitol gate." She looks through the large bay window.

"Where you're standing is where I observe the crowds streaming in to attend Heimbal's festivals. It's quite a sight, especially when the gate is closed and the remaining mob is refused entry. Herasians become hysterical."

"I know. The festivals are addictive." She turns to relax on some floor cushions, then gets to the point of our meeting: "The disappearances are new to Balam. They didn't occur during Heimbal's first reign."

"How can you be sure?"

"I've been doing research on Herasian history since I came here, in particular looking up the history of Balam and asking experts on cult protocol if the present practice is the same as in ages past. They all answer that it is, except for calling forth the 'prepared' from among the festival goers. It's as though the cult has undergone a mutation, so to speak, since those early days. Apart from Heimbal's forced expulsion to Degras, do you know of anything that could have caused a change?"

"Um-hum," I nod slowly.

"Please tell me!"

"Ah...well, this may sound strange, but do you remember I told you while on Degras I saw aliens, giants, mummified in an underground chamber?"

"Yes."

"...They're here."

Maiori is silent for a moment, raises her eyebrows and responds: "That's strange alright, that Heimbal should bother to transport two dead aliens with him, but I don't see why..."

"No! They're not dead. They're alive, here on Heras. I saw them myself."

"What?"

"That's right! I'm really not surprised, having seen the advanced technology in their possession, keeping Heimbal's awareness alive, and all. It wouldn't be reasonable for them not to practice their survival sciences on their own behalf."

"But how did you see them on Heras?"

"Heimbal insisted that I meet them. I'll never forget it. I

was escorted by priests carrying torches down a long tunnel of stairs, to a stone chamber far under the Capitol. The two creatures sat motionless on stone chairs that gave the impression of thrones. They're monsters. Each has only one eye, set in a diaphragm in the middle of its forehead, above its flat nose. Their mouths are small and round, and protrude from their swollen faces. There's no hair. The whole hideous arrangement is planted on a tremendous bulk covered from the neck down by a slick garment. They made no sound, but observed me with minds that gave the sensation of a trial where my worth was being judged. Despite my fear I must have made a favorable impression. That's when Heimbal conveyed that they were in favor of my appointment as Minister of Defence. It's a sensitive post for one who's not a member of the Balam cult."

"Hmmm...." Maiori thinks for a moment, then responds: "Since both the disappearances from the festivals and these aliens are new to Balam, it's logical to suspect a connection between the two. What's particularly interesting is that the revellers are tested with aura-scanners. When I was last on Aesiris there was research being done on life's aura. Strange findings came to light concerning aura transference."

"You mean one life form taking over the aura of another?"

"Yes. Of course, it doesn't happen naturally. We researchers found an artificial method to provoke the transference. The result on the donor was immediate aging depending on the amount of aura loss, while the result on the recipient was a marked rejuvenation."

I pause for a moment to think about the discovery. "Are you suggesting that the giants live off the auras of the disappeared from the festivals?"

"That's my guess. It would be very natural for them to require some form of aura transference after lying dormant for...

who knows how long? It explains Heimbal's connection with them too. They're using the Balam devoted and Heimbal's control over them as a source of supply."

The weight of Maiori's theory presses on me. "That doesn't explain why the victims are taken during the festivals."

"On the contrary. It's known that one's aura isn't stable; it changes with the emotional state. If the Balam devotees are taken at the height of the festivals some efficiency is introduced into the selection of victims."

I lower myself slowly to a sitting position to contemplate the whole idea. "Maiori, you may have resolved the mystery at that. I wondered what the giants' connection was with Heimbal, and why they'd be interested in Kolaria at all. If adventurers or explorers they wouldn't have been content to lay dormant on Degras, hidden from the universe. It seems more likely that they were avoiding pursuers, and not just the Veradi."

"They're dangerous, Lucirin."

I have to agree. On how many life forms across the galaxy have the giants practiced their craft? Could they be hunted by other species over the bounds of space for this crime? "I suppose you think we should help Heimbal rid Balam of these parasites." My remark receives no response from Maiori, who stares at me with vacant eyes. "Don't you?" I insist.

"Well...I'm not at all certain Heimbal wishes to rid himself of the giants," she finally responds.

I'm puzzled by her uncharacteristic stance. "Isn't it obvious? They prey upon his following. Every leader has a moral obligation to protect his following."

"I'm not sure Heimbal feels any moral obligation whatever. Remember, if you are correct in believing that Heimbal today is merely the mechanized memory of what was once a human being, there's no guarantee that morality circuitry was built into the machine, only memory and intelligence."

"True, there's no guarantee, but I do know the machine uses logic, and what is morality except a behavioural pattern adapted to survival? The machine would have to arrive at the same conclusion by logical deduction as it would by moral sentiment. After all, what could be more obvious as a logical deduction than the need of a leader to protect his following for the sake of mutual survival?"

"Then what of the orgy at every thirty-eight day interval? Where is the logic in it that facilitates life for Herasians and makes survival more certain for them? You've seen the effects on the people yourself. Many have forsaken the old code given them by the Aesir. They no longer strive toward any fulfilment in life whatever, but have their thoughts centered around each festival."

The shallowness of Maiori's criticism fills me with indignation. "Don't you see? Herasians no longer have to be concerned with survival. With the technical benefits I've given them their lives have been eased beyond their wildest expectations. They no longer have to plough, shovel, push and haul; material wants can now be satisfied with thought impressions, like on Aesiris, and I plan much more for them once the Aesir threat is over. They'll enjoy life to the fullest."

"Oh, Lucirin," she sighs, "where can I begin? Your early years on Aesiris were filled with technical matters; you were never a good student when it came to the life sciences. I, on the other hand, specialized as expected in that learning, and I can tell you that regardless of all the wonderful new gadgets and way-of-life you've supplied Herasians, their world is doomed."

"How can that be?" I ask with an incredulous scowl. "When people's lives improve it signals a healthy, progressive society, not doom!"

"The point I wish to make is that you have taken striving out of the lives of Herasians. Only an intellectual people can withstand the impact of vast material improvement, because they can then occupy their lives with work of the mind. Without those native qualities people are lost; they have nothing to occupy their time and drift into the sterile search for pleasure that has obviously become prevalent on this planet with the introduction of your tools."

"And what is wrong with people enjoying life to the fullest?" I ask provocatively since it is obvious that Maiori has been thoroughly indoctrinated with the anti-freedom and anti-life philosophy of the Veradi.

"Without dedication people can lapse into the frivolity of living life for itself, especially if given technical devices for easing their burdens. I can see no such dedication solicited by Balam. Heimbal is not interested in genuinely improving the lives of Herasians. As a former leader he was interested only in accumulating power, and found a means to that end with the invention of telepathic hypnosis, an invention that was most effective on the simple Herasians who never forgot the bliss he could instil, and eulogized him ever after. Heimbal's circuits, whether transferred to a machine or not, still discharge in the same pattern; the drive is for power, and he will sacrifice even his own followers for that fulfilment. The arrangement is simple: he feeds the giant aliens and they ensure his android supremacy."

Maiori's sophistry kindles a spark of anger in my breast, the first I have ever felt toward her. Searching for an answer against her Veradi inspired fanaticism, I can only retort: "Such unfounded suspicion of Heimbal is unjustified. He may be manipulative but he *is* a great religious leader. It's a mistake to confuse the weaknesses of the man for his weaknesses as a leader. As for Herasians, they are people. Just on that basis they have a perfect right to all the conveniences, the longevity and material satisfaction that can be provided by Aesir technology. Is that so difficult to understand, Maiori, by one as humane as yourself? Or have you been so warped and twisted by the Veradi Belief that you've lost all humanitarian sentiment?"

My remarks make no impression on Maiori. She continues to think with the cool callousness of an Aesir: "The elevation of 'people' to supreme position in an individual's value system signifies the loss of dedication in that individual. He or she feels no superior goals above the level of life for its own sake, whereas we Aesir know that the living of life is secondary to the advancing of life. The perversion of philosophical principles is evident in what you have said, Lucirin, because if I read you correctly, you are more interested in furthering your popularity among the population with your gifts than being motivated from genuine humanitarian concern.

"There's evidently a wide gap in our thinking," she continues. "I'm surprised there should be, since your early development was on Aesiris and you must have been influenced by the Veradi as I was. Perhaps I'm seeing you correctly for the first time, for it is now evident to me that you have deliberately chosen the opposite path to the Belief."

"Of course! The Veradi are tyrants over the mind more than over the body. My ambition is to cast off that tyranny."

She quietly looks at me with a knowledgeable smile. "You've always been good at rationalizing your motives. No, Lucirin, you know that society needs structure as well as freedom, that the duration of civilization is in fact impossible without devotion to a Cause of one sort or another, and that without it social entropy is inevitable. For us, the Belief of the Veradi provides that structure. But you have shunned the Aesir Belief for your own base ambitions, and have deliberately not understood its glorious doctrine. Yes, you are a Herasian by nature. Whereas Heimbal offers the narcotic of his festivals you are caught in a senseless narcotic too, the narcotic of ignorance, because truth is too painful for you."

I'm aghast: "I've spent years in learning..."

"Yes, learning, not understanding. Lucirin, let's leave, just the two of us, and seek out a new life somewhere else, perhaps beyond Kolaria. Or are you so influenced by Balam that you would not want to leave?"

"Fleeing is an illusion. Our place is here, where we can live in freedom and plenty, and we can do that once the Veradi tyranny is no more."

"I now see how strongly you feel. How you have changed! I remember when you were proud of Aesiris, and proud to be Aesir."

Her remark burns into me. It is true, I was proud, I *am* proud, to be Aesir, regardless of all I say and feel against the Veradi. "You've misread my motives. My struggle has never been against Aesiris as such, but against the Veradi and their twisted Belief. I consider it my duty to rid Kolaria of their cold hand. *They* are the traitors against Aesiris, indeed, they are psychopaths who oppress all that is natural in the human breast."

"Look at it practically. Whether or not it's only the Veradi you wish to overcome, Heras is now in a vicious struggle with Aesiris. Do you really think this puny world can win? You have survived this long only because the Aesir are rebuilding their fleet, and when that fleet is constructed what chance will you really have?"

"Yes, I know perfectly well we are only in a lull between belligerencies. They haven't struck back because of our own repaired fleet. Fortunately we can repair ships faster than they can build them. But I know time is on their side, and we must strike at them before they have a fully rebuilt fleet. We cannot simply wait for them to strike at us."

"Heras overpowering Aesiris. I can't imagine it."

"Aesiris is not without its weaknesses, being a world artificially contrived. We need only destroy its polar dikes and the planet will revert to its original, sterile condition. And our restored fleet is not the only reason for hope of wrestling Herasian freedom: our ships possess a technical device of which the Aesir are ignorant: a 'blind' that can make them invisible."

"I've never heard of such a device."

"Neither did I, until I met the aliens. That was another reason for our meeting under the Capitol, to give me the technical instructions for it. Conceptually the idea is simple: it bends light around the object not meant to be seen. When that light is of a ship's background, say a blue sky, the ship becomes virtually invisible."

"Such an appropriate device for fleeing avengers! As would be their control over the life processes for interstellar travel!"

"With our repaired fleet of captured vessels, and our 'blind' technology donated by the aliens, Aesiris' dikes look very vulnerable."

"Lucirin, you have embarked on a very dangerous course, not only for yourself but for all Kolaria. I guarantee the death of Aesiris would bring destruction on everyone."

"You needn't worry that will happen. Heimbal is not so foolish to destroy wealth. He would like to take Aesiris intact, to enhance his own power. During my days on Aesiris, part of my studies was in military matters. At that time I was concerned about defence, thinking as Rasan such information would be important. It should be no surprise that I found Aesiris to be most vulnerable at its dikes, so I took upon myself the task of finding the most vulnerable section, and found it, at sluice twelve of both dikes. A dozen or so annihilator discharges from a star cruiser would be enough to make each dike collapse. I'm doubtful if the Veradi know about this, since I discovered it by chance after prolonged examination of plans left by the Tsia. The revelation of dike weakness and the threat of our 'blind' will be sufficient to have the planet surrendered intact."

"And if it isn't?"

"I have no doubt the Veradi will yield. They are cowards in my estimation and when they realize the threat they face, the uncertainty and shock will be terrifying."

"Lucirin, I wish I could support you in this wild ambition, but I do not. Your reasoning is emotional, and Herasian. I guess my eyes are finally opened to your true Herasian nature. I'm sorry."

Maiori leaves my quarters in distress, although she bears under it bravely. I do not see her again until days later when I receive a message from her handmaid of a grave illness that has come over her. "Campora," reads the message, the deadly disease of Gahes that crystallizes the salts and minerals of the body to eventually petrify its victim into a solid statue of stone. I rush to Maiori's quarters to see her encapsulated under a quarantine canopy. Her eyes, sunken under dark, swollen lids, already give the first telltale sign of the dreaded malady.

"How could she contact Campora on Heras?" I ask her handmaid, a gaunt, thin woman dressed in black. "The disease has never been known here."

"Maiori was on Gahes and spent more than her quota of time there in the open. She was not prepared against all the Gahean sicknesses."

"That was a long time ago. Why should it strike now?"

"Sometimes Campora strikes not at all, even though one

carries it in the blood. That's a feature of Campora. After it infects you never know when it will strike."

"Maiori will have the best physicians on Heras."

"Heras has no physicians of merit left," she comments dryly. "They left after the revolution. There's only one chance she has to be cured: by returning to Aesiris."

Leaning against the capsule I see how the disease has already taken its effect. The flesh of her face has turned yellow, her hair, that once gleamed in the Aesir sunlight, has lost its lustre. "Aesiris it is," I tell her handmaid. "I'll have a carrier summoned right away."

With my last words Maiori rolls her head to the side for a better view, releasing a tear that moistens her pillow. "Goodbye, Lucirin," she says in a voice that is barely audible.

Days later Arrana hears of Maiori's departure and storms into my quarters. "You silver eared idiot!" she yells. "Can you be so dumb not to know she'll warn Aesir of our plans?"

"I'm aware she now has that opportunity," I coolly respond from my position on a favorite reposer. "I'm also aware she can tell the Veradi of our repaired fleet and of the discipline I inspire in our troops. Knowledge like that will produce dread in the hearts of the Veradi, dread that will be advantageous to our strategy."

"A lot of use your strategy be now," she snorts. "You want to save Aesiris. That's hopeless with Maiori returned. I say we put an end to Aesiris, good and sure."

"Be calm, Arrana. Maiori is loyal to me. She would like to see me restored to my rightful position, even to the post of Rasan."

"Is that so? Now let me reveal something to you! I did a little snoop on your precious Maiori, and found the old wart she has for a handmaid was a member of the Quareg gentry."

"There's nothing odd about that. It would be natural for Maiori to request someone with class around her instead of an uncouth wench from the fields."

"We're talking about loyalties, my dear," she snarls in her sarcastic tone. "That woman's family lost property with the Revolt; her feelings are with Aesiris and she'd send a lying note if your Maiori wanted it, nor would the old hag hesitate with a scheme to leave Heras. As for Maiori, is she not wise about malaise? Could she not feign the look of Campora in a manner that would fool the most knowledgeable physician?"

"Your insinuations are baseless."

"Baseless! Was it only by chance she fell ill now, when we prepared our final scathe? I tell you, those poor fools you send to the polar dikes will be captives the moment they reach Aesiris!"

With her last comment I look on Arrana in silence, a silence that conveys full meaning to her.

"Oh no!" she gasps. "Not us!"

"I've already notified Heimbal of the plan. He and his alien friends are in favor of saving Aesiris from destruction if that is possible. They make only one demand, that it is we with 0-7-1 that present the threat to the Veradi. Their reasoning is that I'm already most familiar with Aesiris and possible Veradi reactions. Should your fear be realized and we are captured, Heimbal will strike soon after, with his full invasion force."

"Another gamble," she says, her tone becoming more despairing. "You trust Heimbal for sure? From what I see, you outlived your use on Heras, and your hungry nature makes you a threat, of that he is aware. It would suit his purpose nicely if Aesir saved him the trouble of both our scathes."

Arrana provokes me to laugh, a gesture that does nothing to ease her anger. "What a wily wench you are! Yes, I'm aware that our days on Heras are numbered. That's the reason I insisted on this tactic. Should the Veradi succumb to our threat, I'll demand the Rasan's authority for myself, not for Heimbal."

"And if the Veradi are not so generous?"

"Their capitulation will be easier If made to me, a former Aesir, not Heimbal, but..." I shrug with the acknowledgement, "it *will* be an act of desperation, agreed. Arrana, we've been in desperate situations before, and I've never caused you to grieve your decision to join with me."

"There's always a first time!" she responds, striding toward the exit. When angered like this, dressed in her tight fitting, dark uniform, her flaming hair flung loose and eyes flashing, she presents a formidable countenance. Reaching the masonry she rests her upper frame against curled fingers at neck level, twists a strong, shapely body in my direction, and with her menacing smile adds: "But since the only other choice is a dire fate on Heras, I and my followers will join you in that exploit." Then with levelled eyes, adds: "Besides, it will be a real pleasure to see a grand fool like you in Aesir bondage." She throws her head back arrogantly and with one stride disappears past the doorway.

14

RETURN

Aᴇsɪʀɪs has a special fascination for those who gaze upon it for the first time. As we approach, the growing image sparks excitement that shakes away the last vestiges of hibernation sleep.

"There's a sight I never thought to see," says a voice from the darkness.

"It shines like a jewel in the void," says another.

The light from our viewer's bubble makes a play of moving shadow on the well-sculptured shapes of my companions. We are a ship's crew of twelve, watching the glittering orb from the blackness of our control chamber.

"HOW FORTUNATE HUMANS ARE, TO SPEND LONG, BORING FLIGHTS IN PEACEFUL OBLIVION. NOW I, BESIDES THE WORK OF FLIGHT CORRECTION, HAVE HAD TO CONTENT MYSELF WITH CALCULATIONS, SOME OF WHICH WILL BE OF INTEREST TO YOU, CAPTAIN."

"Let's hear them."

"THEY DETERMINE THE EFFECTIVENESS OF OUR 'BLIND'. IF THE AESIR USE NO DEFENSIVE FLIGHT PATTERN WE HAVE INFINITE ADVANTAGE, BUT IF THEY USE A HEXAHEDRON FORMATION THE SACRIFICE OF ONE OF THEIR SHIPS ALLOWS THE REMAINING TO CALCULATE OUR POSITION FASTER THAN THE TIME WE WOULD TAKE TO ESCAPE."

"That's certainly pertinent information, 0-7-1. I don't want to engage the Aesir, but if something goes wrong..."

"IT WOULD BE MOST DANGEROUS. THE DIFFICULTY IS: ALTHOUGH WE CAN BE CONCEALED OUR ANNIHILATOR DISCHARGE CANNOT BE."

"Where's our fleet?"

"IT IS STILL ON HERAS."

"That's strange. They should be en route."

Arrana smirks. "Like I told you, Heimbal sent us here for riddance."

"0-7-1, where's the Aesir fleet?"

"IT IS EN ROUTE TO HERAS. WE PASSED IT WHILE YOU WERE IN HIBERNATION. I MIGHT ADD, CAPTAIN, IT WAS ORGANIZED IN HEXAHEDRONAL PATTERNS."

"Then there's no doubt: the Aesir are aware of the 'blind'. They've already devised protective measures."

"YES, CAPTAIN."

Arrana stares at me contemptuously. "You told Maiori of the 'blind'?"

"I did, but I'm confident the Aesir already knew about it from ages past. At least they knew of the aliens who invented it. I found that out during the party at the Capitol, and no doubt they encountered the 'blind' in their ancient war against Balam. If anyone deserves our anger it's Heimbal. He and his alien friends knew of the Aesir defence but allowed us to proceed, thinking we would engage Aesir ships in their protective formation. What he didn't consider was the updating in flight-ship technology over the centuries, that volunteered 0-7-1's calculation."

Arrana is distraught: "Now there be two fleets that threaten us, the Herasian as well as Aesir."

"That's true. Let's hope they obliterate each other. All that work, though, that we put into restoring the Herasian fleet, only to have it turn against us. I must say, life has its ironies."

We scan Aesiris for remaining ships. Small groups are spotted guarding the polar dikes. Each group is composed of a triangle of three ships with a ship above and another below the plane of the triangle, making a five pointed 'diamond' of six imaginary faces: a hexahedron.

"This is a mess you've led us into. We're here without support, we dare not finish our task because of Aesir defence, and we can't return to Heras because Heimbal revealed his hand. Did I forget anything?"

At times Arrana can be most irritating. I sit quietly, contemplating my old lesson on adversity and survival; there *must* be a resolution possible. Finally I turn to her: "Heimbal is not as clever as he thinks. He's placed us in a better position for our own purpose than if we were encumbered by his fleet. Instead of threatening from behind the 'blind' we'll use solar bombs, remotely activated."

"And how do you figure *that?*"

"We'll disembark at each dike using cephalo-shields to avoid detection, plant the devices, then on the threat of blowing up the dikes by remote command, demand new imprinting for the Aesir ships and place our own crew members in charge. Any excess ships can be destroyed. That will give us control of the planet. We don't need Heimbal's fleet."

"You mean expose ourselves on the ground to plant explosives? Events will move quickly, and I'm not forgetting the Veradi are warned of our little venture here."

"You needn't worry about Maiori. She's aware of Veradi injustice and would like to see my return."

She bellows: "Your fancy with that woman blinds you! I assure we'll be seized the moment we set foot on Aesiris!"

"What other course is there? We can't go back and we can't go forward without taking risks."

"How many of us will be on the ground?"

"All hands will make the work go faster. Each explosive will have to be hidden under the rubble. We'll need everyone to help remove and replace those rocks."

"Then 0-7-1 will be left in self command?"

"Yes."

She turns to our flight-ship: "0-7-1, I now give you instruction if present mission fails: your first duty must be the wasting of the dikes by annihilator. Take all precautions to avoid your own scathe, but you destroy the dikes."

"IF I UNDERSTAND YOU CORRECTLY, ARRANA, YOU ARE GIVING ME A FIRST PRIORITY ORDER TO DESTROY THE DIKES IF YOUR MISSION ON THE SURFACE FAILS."

"That's what I said."

"FIRST COMMAND AUTHORIZATION REQUIRED."

"What? You dumb pile of metal!"

"0-7-1 means I must confirm the order because of its consequences if executed. My intention with the solar bombs is only to threaten the Veradi into capitulation."

"Yes, my dear Captain," she responds with her icy smirk. "We all know you don't want your beautiful Aesiris in total ruin. But you said yourself there be no danger of our capture, even with Maiori returned. So why hesitate?"

"Our flight-ship is concerned because Aesiris is completely dependent on those dikes. If they're destroyed the planet will have no available water. It will drain into caverns deep underground. All vegetation will die. Life-supporting oxygen will eventually disappear from the atmosphere. Aesiris will revert to its primordial state: a world unfit for habitation."

Her eyes are hard as steel. "Confirm the order or you need not expect me or my followers on that soil!" She is adamant, but cowing the Veradi into yielding is our only hope. I override 0-7-1's concern and confirm the order.

"FIRST PRIORITY ORDER WILL BE EXECUTED UNDER INDICATED CIRCUMSTANCES."

Our viewer displays areas of rich foliage interspersed with vertical rock mountains, shinning canals, domes of domestic habitats, sleek research structures and scattered art centers interconnected by winding walkways, all of which give way to the stark southern desert and finally the dike of the south polar sea. We skirt its base where 0-7-1 releases the first charge for installation, then departs without crew to return when we have finished.

Not forgetting our cephalo-shields to avoid detection, we scurry between huge boulders, barely taking notice of the massive dike walls towering above us. High overhead, the tormented, storm-tossed sea rages in marked contrast to the desert terrain where we work. A river of water hurtles from the sluice into a major canal, producing a fine mist and perpetual dampness on the rocks where we carry the charge. Slipperiness increases our need for care. A giant number '12' is inscribed on the dike above the sluice. We carry our first bomb through crevasses between the mountainous rubble, installing it deep at the base of a ravine formed by a pile of overlaying granite, to help direct the blast into the dike.

We emerge from the rocks into the open when I turn to congratulate my companions: "That didn't take long. Now for the next char..."

The whine of their motors could not be heard over the roar of the sluice. The sight of them is without warning. Above are vul-canae: five, in the diamond formation predicted by 0-7-1!

"CEASE ACTIVITIES!" blares a voice from a hovering craft.

Arransin splinter, fleeing in panic. "No!" I cry, "Come back!" but it's too late. The 'crack' of annihilators tears the air. Two of my companions disappear in their own vapor; the others halt in terror.

My knees tremble. The area swarms with loyal Herasian guards, all wearing death helmets. Our bomb is quickly removed. The cephalo-shields are yanked from our heads, replaced by those most humiliating instruments of prisoner control, subjectors, clamped to the base of our skulls.

We are ordered toward a transport. Control by subjector is new to Lasha; her walk is stiff and hesitant in her struggle against the electrical manipulations of her captor. "Succumb to the command," I advise. "You can't fight it."

Like errant children we are led away. Most surprising is the swiftness of our capture. Within moments we are herded into the waiting transport, whisked to a flight port adjoining the House of the Veradi, forced to walk across an open area, down a narrow stairwell past a large steel door, into the underground prison of Aesiris. The steel door clangs behind us. Our subjectors are mercifully removed. The jeering guards leave through a rectangular doorway at the opposite end of our cell, energizing a portcullis with their exit. A shocked silence engulfs the stony space.

"Why did I do it? Why did I do it?" Arrana sobs, slowly sinking with her back along the stone wall. "Such a dumb scheme was hopeless from the start." Others of our group sit at the base of the wall, their bodies drooping.

"Our capture happened so rapidly," I lament. "One moment everything was going as planned, the next moment we're in prison."

"Pthaa!" Arrana sputters, her look changing from despair to disgust. "Don't tell me you're surprised. You bungler! But you're correct on one thing: our capture happened fast, *too* fast. Now you don't suppose your darling Maiori had anything to do with it?"

"Absolutely not!" but my voice has a quiver. "We were caught by chance, by a patrol."

"A patrol," she snickers. "We wore your shields. How did they find us? So fast! So easily! As if they were waiting for saboteurs! In the very spot where we struck! Huh?"

Maiori, a traitor! The thought is sickening. I too now slide down the wall of our confinement, and remain on the floor in silence, joining the despair of the group. Finally I turn: "Arrana, what I did was the only possibility left open to us. Heras was becoming too dangerous; perhaps all Kolaria would be too dangerous if Heimbal and his aliens gained victory over Aesiris. It was far better to take a chance the way we did."

Arrana looks up at the bleak ceiling, sighs and presses the back of her head against the stone. "That's not my vex. I'm angered because you're such a fool."

"Maiori?"

"Of course!"

Silence again envelopes the cell, broken shortly by the sound of approaching footsteps. The doorway's portcullis is interrupted with the entrance of a Veradi flanked by two officials and a score of guards.

"Prisoners will acknowledge Veradi Navis."

We remain seated. Two guards yank me to my feet, another keeps his helmet trained in my direction, its front diaphragm open, exposing its lethal orifice. One thought impression of this guard and I'll be nothing but a column of smoke and a memory.

A Herasian guard, intimidated by the presence of the Veradi, snaps to attention. "The infamous Lucirin, twenty-nine Andra-naudae, your Eminence."

The Veradi's finger gestures in my direction: "Bring him to the questioning chamber."

A subjector is clamped to my neck for the Veradi's safety. I am led into a sparsely furnished room accompanied by the Veradi and her two officials. They take seats, I remain standing. A cephalo-scanner verifies my identity.

"This is not a trial, Lucirin," Navis begins. "You already had your trial twenty-six Aesiris years ago. I remember it. I was there. Apparently your nature has been changed very little by your stay on Gahes, short as it was."

"If this isn't a trial, what is it?"

"Merely a formality." She relaxes her elbows on the rests of her seat and leisurely dovetails her fingers before her at neck level. "We don't think it proper to terminate a life without allowing the prisoner a last chance to speak his mind. Perhaps there is something you will say that will change the sentence."

"Ah! At last the Veradi have summoned enough fortitude for my execution instead of sending me to die in a vermin infested swamp."

My statement causes Navis to lower her piercing eyes. "With certainty, our policy of sending gifted undesirables to the Gahean swamp is not the most noble, but entirely understandable if such men as you are likely to escape when the least generosity is shown them."

"What you mean to say is that the policy is one of expediency, not justice. It's merely a means of taking the direct guilt of blood off your hands when your victim has never committed a crime. You conniving cowards! Your Belief is not prepared for those of noble and innovative character who can withstand its penalties, so you are forced to invent a little extra."

Navis springs to her feet, followed instantly by her two officials. "Reproach the Veradi if you wish, but I'll have you know the sacred tenets of the Belief are beyond the admonishments of one such as you. This interview is ended."

"Ended? It has hardly begun!"

"You have yourself to blame for its short duration. I see nothing in your 'noble and innovative character' that entitles you to any concessions whatever. Your execution will take place with the end of your companions' trails. You may not be alone."

"They're to be tried, not given a...'formality'?"

"Yes," is the curt answer.

I am ordered back to the cell. My companions are selected one after another, their trials taking considerable time. The first is to be returned to Gahes; then the second, also to Gahes. Arrana is called out. When she returns her face is flush, apparently from a rage, and I know the trial did not go well for her. "Execution!" she snaps. Finally at the end of our third full day of confinement the last member of our party returns. Of our ship's remaining crew only Arrana and I are to face execution, the rest are to be returned to Gahes.

The Aesir method of execution is brutally simple. The victim is taken into the desert, away from the population, and there evaporated by annihilator.

On the day after the trials our small band is separated. Our faithful companions are led up the stairwell of our cell through the steel door, all with distressed faces and tear-laden eyes for the fate that awaits Arrana and me. A bright stream of sunlight through the open door livens our prison, yet with the exit of our friends the hollowness adds a new dimension to our depression.

The wait is short. A squad of Herasian guards enters. *How typical of the Aesir, to have Herasians do their dirty work.* One of the men approaches us directly, carrying two subjectors and clamps one each to the back of our necks.

Arrana and I are led up the stairwell into the warm brightness, across the flight port to a waiting old cargo transporter. We are directed to sit next to a small port window, with the guards taking positions along the opposite wall of the cargo bay. An undisciplined band of brigands, they have the insolence to stare, some even with laughter and rude gestures. To avoid their vulgarity I direct my gaze to the transporter in feigned interest. It is an ancient craft, amply endowed with the filth of use, and possibly drawn into service by these Herasians to increase our humiliation.

We pass a few brisk moments of flight over the tree-enshrouded countryside of Aesiris. Watching the panorama through the port window, I observe my last sights: the vast cultivated jungles punctured by protruding mesas, where as a boy I delighted. I cannot help reflecting that all my delights and joys in life are about to come to a quick end in one blinding flash. Was it worth the risk? Yes. My mistakes were not so bad; anyone can make them when betrayed, and I was betrayed not once, but twice. Besides the betrayal of Heimbal there was the betrayal of Maiori, which I am now forced to admit. Thus, in addition to the Veradi, the known enemy in front, there was the unknown behind.

The transporter passes from the forest regions to the southern desert and lands. Arrana and I walk unhurriedly down its ramp into the waiting circle of Herasian guards. Now constrained by the threat from the annihilators, our subjectors are removed to not be wasted in our executioners' blast.

The air is cool at this latitude. Before us is a mesa, an imposing natural structure of solid stone reaching into the sky. A drift of cloud hangs onto its leeward side. In the distance are the high, massive walls of the southern dike. Electric storms rumble over the polar sea behind. The commander of our execution squad is an old Herasian with a limp, who wears a biological prosthesis that did not adhere adequately to his leg, possibly due to age. He may have lost his leg in our Revolt. "Walk twenty paces," he orders, "then wait. We still have to receive the final yea for your executions."

We walk the twenty paces with a leisurely gait. My heart

pounds. We suppress our instinct to flee because we have both resolved not to disgrace ourselves by a futile act of cowardice.

"That's far enough. Turn and face the squad, if you want," the leader shouts.

We now wait, for how long I don't know. The guards appear relaxed but keep us under strict observation. None remove their helmets, the instruments of our executions.

"There's something strange about this," I tell Arrana. "Why the delay? I know for certain the Veradi want my death." I suddenly realize that what they really want is our flight-ship; without it we are powerless but it continues to pose a danger.

"I see Aesir ships over the dike," Arrana motions. "They still fret about 0-7-1."

"Look at the dike, Arrana, we're in view of sluice twelve." She continues squinting into the distance to see the large number etched above the sluice. "Could it be just a coincidence they brought us to this location?"

"Why would they care? It's no matter to them where they finish us."

"That's what makes me wonder, unless it's to make us more visible to 0-7-1, being close to the weak section where they know 0-7-1 should strike."

"You think they *want* 0-7-1 to know we're here?"

"I do. The question is: why?"

"But aren't they bothered about our rescue?"

"Putting things together, my guess is that's exactly what they want 0-7-1 to do. We're bait. Our Herasian guards have no idea, but their transporter probably carries a bomb that will blast everything to atoms, including us and 0-7-1, if it is attacked."

Her eyes widen. "Those devils! They sacrifice their loyal folk."

"That's why there's not one Aesir on board. They're all

Herasian, including the commander. I wondered about that.
You would think with dangerous celebrities like us there would
be at least one, if for no other reason than to confirm our
executions."

"When will it happen?"

"Our wait shouldn't be long. Either way we lose: if the Aesir
succeed in destroying 0-7-1, those guards will vaporize us,
and if 0-7-1 tries rescuing us, everyone here will be blown to
pieces."

The morning passes. We've grown weary and have seated
ourselves on a sizeable boulder protruding from the dry soil.
The ships protecting the dike leave. "They're taking a chance,"
I mention, pointing to the departing specks in the distance.
"They feel confident their attempts at remotely neutralizing 0-
7-1 have succeeded. It's another test."

We wait more. The strain begins to tell on Arrana. "I'd prefer they finish us and be through," she grumbles.

I embrace her. "With those departed ships the Aesir gave
0-7-1 an increased incentive to rescue us. Since it has not with
no warrior ship within range of helping, that strongly indicates
their success in neutralizing its imprinting. They feel safe."

The Herasian commander storms out of the transporter:
"Attention! Attention! On your feet! Firing positions!" There's
urgency in his voice. The guards grudgingly rise and stumble
into their positions. My thoughts are that this is certainly the
end, my final moments, when the bright flash of annihilator
lights the horizon. Hammering sounds roll from the distance.
The ill-trained guards cannot resist the look back. Repetitive
rays streak back and forth across the dike. "Attention!
Attention!" the commander shouts, but the guards are clearly
nervous. Then it happens: the weakened dike explodes from the
pressure behind, spewing huge chunks of stone in a monstrous

gush. Onrushing water gorges into the dry soil, loosening rocks with its impact, sweeping them into its mud-laden torrents. A tidal wave approaches!

"Water!" a guard yells.

"Run!" I needlessly shout to Arrana who has already begun to scamper. The guards are thrown into confusion between our sudden escape and their awe of the spectacle behind. They jostle each other, some trying to reach their transporter, others firing wildly in our direction.

Pent up adrenaline allows bounding strides over the rock-strewn terrain. Our exertion soon puts us beyond danger from the guards' erratic fire; our fear now is drowning in the frothing brown rush. Foolishly we try to outrun its approach. The ground trembles underfoot from the oncoming wave. We near exhaustion from strain and fright; my heart pounds as if to jump from my chest, when a shape hovers overhead. At first I think it is the Aesir transporter, but no! It advances ahead with its belly diaphragm open. 0-7-1 has come to our rescue. We scramble inside and the ship resumes its 'blind'.

A look at the viewer reveals the transporter. The water is now upon it, yet its portal is still open and its access ramp is congested with guards. They're yelling and flailing. The mighty onrush capsizes it, spills over its hull and gouges into the base of the nearby hill.

Between gasps, I ask our flight-ship: "0-7-1...have you destroyed...the north dike?"

"YES, CAPTAIN."

"Let's see it."

The north plain is a vast expanse of mud awash with torrents of water. A great gash is in the dike, from which the life-sustaining fluid is still draining. It soaks into the parched soil, giving a scene of muddy desolation.

"This is for certain the death of Aesiris," I tell Arrana. The horror of the realization presses on me. I owe my life to what I am witnessing. It is the inevitable, if unintended, culmination of everything I have been striving to accomplish, but as I gaze upon that destruction I feel no triumph, no sense of achievement, only a great emptiness for what it means.

" DEFENDING SHIPS HAVE RETURNED."

Our viewer shows the Aesir vul-canae flying in their formations over the emptying bowl of what was once a polar sea. They'll search in vain for their planet's destroyers. I have no intention of testing our 'blind' against their clever pattern.

"I MIGHT COMMENT, CAPTAIN, THE AESIR FAILED BECAUSE THEY UNDERESTIMATED MY DEDICATION TO YOUR CAUSE. THEY TRIED NUMEROUS ATTEMPTS TO CANCEL MY IMPRINTING BY REMOTE COMMAND. WHEN I DID NOT ATTACK OR ATTEMPT A RESCUE THEY LEFT THEIR STATIONS. BUT YOU HAVE DONE A MASTERFUL JOB AT IMPRINTING."

"Thank you, 0-7-1." My voice is barely audible.

"ARE YOU ALRIGHT, CAPTAIN? YOU SEEM DISTRACTED."

"Oh! Yes...I'm...I'm just overwhelmed by the sight." My thoughts continue, still in a restrained voice: "All this destruction is caused by more than anything we've done. The Aesir themselves are responsible. They were over confident. Being masters for so long it was inconceivable to them that their world could ever be seriously threatened. It's the same callousness we saw at the Capitol flight port." Regaining composure: "Now a question: you had all morning to rescue us from our execution squad. Why didn't you?"

"YOU FORGET MY FIRST PRIORITY ORDER."

Arrana is perplexed. "What links my order with your tarry to our rescue? That for sure was more important than the dikes!"

"Not to the machine mind," I explain. "By giving 0-7-1 a

first priority order to destroy the dikes in event of our capture, you inadvertently overrode its decision-making circuits. Its *first* objective had to be to destroy the dikes. We're lucky it did, or it would have attacked the transporter and destroyed us all."

"Machine logic!" she sneers.

Days pass. We keep Aesiris under constant observation. A large fleet of transports mysteriously lifts from the surface and heads for an unknown destination. The next day we take a closer look, employing life detection probes continually.

"Nothing! Arrana, our detectors are sensing no remaining human life on the planet!"

"They went with the fleet."

"That fleet wasn't nearly big enough to accommodate the whole population of Aesiris. Something strange has happened."

We coast slowly over the surface to observe the damage we've wrought upon this once magnificent world. Forests are already changing color in the tropical heat of Aesiris' suns. Canals, normally sparkling with water, are dry, exposing their bottoms like white bones of aged skeletons. We skirt the centers of research and creativity; their dark interiors stare back through hollow apertures. No activity is in any habitat, normally bustling with youth. *We observe a dead world.*

We disembark at the House of the Veradi. As we enter the grandiose structure, memories from my past overcome me, except now how different with the hollowness, without the busy councillors, teachers, philosophers, social strategists and scholars passing to and fro. How strange the silence instead of the cacophony of voices and gurgling fountains. To be heard are only the sounds of our footsteps echoing against the high arches and lofty sculptures, the latter looking down on us in resigned arrogance. Without its inmates, that gave the House its life, even the masterpieces of mosaic and painting, seen in profusion, lose their meaning and cast a pall of bland impotence. "How will we find the Council Chamber?" Arrana whispers, the deathly stillness demanding reverence for the sanctity of the House, even from its destroyers.

Our roaming leads us to an area surrounded by columns, giving access to a wide staircase and an opening directly above. Faint light enters from the opening to our columned area, lending an even glow to the white steps. We slowly climb the stairs, to find the light entering from an elevated row of encircling windows into a cavernous chamber. A high domed ceiling spans the chamber, a chamber that is deathly silent. Arrana, crouching in front of me on the stairs, makes a gesture to stop before entering the voluminous enclosure, then beckons to come forward quietly as she points a rigid finger to *a Veradi seated just beyond the stairwell,* his back toward us. Have we been led into an elaborate trap? We freeze, waiting for any motion, any change of body position, the slightest movement of arm or leg. Nothing! We stealthily move into the vacuous, silent room to see other Veradi visible in the defused light from the high-perched windows. All are seated and motionless. Fixed stares wooden their faces. Our fear and surprise change to wonderment.

Arrana straightens her posture as if in sudden realization and loudly announces: "They all be finished! We enter a Council of dead Veradi!" With that she approaches one of the seated figures, pulls him from his seat and flings him to the floor. The figure retains its seated posture, fixed by *rigor mortis.*

A jittery sigh issues from us both, but our apprehension is replaced by astonishment for the macabre scene we have walked into. The whole chamber is filled with dead Veradi, each cadaver seated as if attending a full session of the Council. By the side of every seat is a goblet: *"Poison!"* I gasp. *"They've all committed suicide!"*

We survey the spectacle of ultimate Veradi defeat in the half-light from the waning afternoon filtering into the spacious extent. Rows and rows of seats are filled with the drained faces: some cadavers look attentive with transfixed, hollow eyes, some have their eyes closed in an expression of resignation, others are almost hidden in the shadows between the silent rows, but all have their heads stretched back as if the rigor of death gave them defiance. On an elevated platform is the Rasan, staring vacantly, his hands clasped on his stomach, and behind him is a wedge of rows containing his special staff, all motionless. I spring up on the platform to better observe the weird sight, hardly believing it. There is Veradi Mayfis, the contemptible wretch whose testimony was responsible for my trial; also Memhin, the presiding Veradi at that trial who gave my sentence, and other members of the inquisition jury, including the twiggy woman who strengthened the charge of heresy.

Usla! The youngest member of the Council, he sits with his face drained, with his fleshy blue hand hanging from his chair to a spilt goblet on the floor. Such an appropriate reward, Usla, for your servile obedience! To imagine that years ago I stood as your victim, sentenced to exile and disgrace because of your testimony — testimony you gave in your groveling curry of the Veradi, only to discover that your sniveling would lead to this end for you and your Council. All this could have been avoided, Usla, if only you had seen me as a liberalizer rather than a threat.

Further along the rows I see Navis, the Veradi who finally sentenced me to death only days ago. Again I marvel in how our fates have changed in so short a time! In the end it is the

Veradi who have succumbed regardless of all their power and cunning. It is I who have triumphed, even from the edge of destruction, but amazing as it all is, I have long known this would happen, as if I were nothing more than a pawn in an incredible destiny.

In exhilaration my attention turns to the dead body of the Rasan. I tear the imperial garland from his head and place it on my own, then dump the body to the floor and take the throne. Surveying the exhibition of death before me, I cannot help but break into uncontrollable, mocking laughter: "I have won! Arrana, I have won!"

She is strangely silent. Unexpectedly she is not sharing my delight. Without comment she motions me to enter one of the vestries adjacent to the Council Chamber. Pale light from the Chamber falls into the room, revealing a crumpled tunic, and from the tunic sprawls a slender arm on the floor, trailing a goblet. I know at once that it is Maiori. There is no trace of Campora. Awakened from my manic trance, I fall on my knees beside the lifeless figure and hold the body to my sobbing chest. My display of grief moves even Arrana to quietly emerge from the shadows. Softly, her hand clasps my shoulder.

15

CABES-TREBLA

DAYS AFTER OUR DISCOVERY of the Veradi suicide we continue searching Aesiris for signs of human life. We find none. Over the entire planet, in habitats and research centers, the same spectre is revealed: mass suicide, of important officials down to third class researchers. Even cybernetic devices have been fused or destroyed. Yet I am convinced the Aesir would not give up so easily, bearing in mind the large fleet of transports we saw leaving.

Presently in the library of the great House, I am joined by Arrana: "Lucirin, why stay so long in this place? It's grim."

"And go where?"

"Anywhere. Kirigna."

Shaking my head: "What we see makes me believe there's no place left in Kolaria for us. It's all been abandoned or destroyed, or soon will be."

Here eyes widen. "Why?"

"The Aesir were a peculiar people, motivated more by ideology than by the needs of survival. Deprived of their mission in life they determined to end that life altogether, and take everything with them. But I think what we see is just the end of a phase, not the total end of the Aesir."

"You're concerned because only the older Aesir committed self scathe."

"Someone was in those ships we saw leaving, obviously of the younger generation who are not found among the suicides.

Now ask yourself why that should be. The older generation could have evacuated to another world of Kolaria if their aim were simply survival. Instead, they chose something quite different. Arrana, those ships were en route to another part of the galaxy, away from Kolaria, to a world so far only the younger Aesir would survive the journey. The older generation would die of old age on the way, and had no mission left in Kolaria, so they made the only decision possible in their moral outlook, suicide, not only on Aesiris but on every colony, and without their technical mastery the colonies of loyal Herasians are suffering the same fate as Aesiris."

"Then we're doomed after all! In spite of all our schemes and plots, our end is sure!"

"Perhaps not."

"You say Heras was destroyed too?"

"Perhaps, but I'm not thinking of Heras or any other world of Kolaria. I'm thinking of Earth."

"Where's Earth? I never heard of the place."

"Earth is the world where our species originated. Its whereabouts in the galaxy is what I hope to learn from this library computer. I suspect the Veradi have known the location of Earth for a long time, and have used that information to chart a course for their émigrés. This computer holds the archives of the House. If I can restore it to use we may learn that location for ourselves."

More days pass, causing Arrana to become restless. She is disturbed by the depression around. A plague of mice has infested the House, where they come to survive a few days longer in one recess or another. The expanse of forest becomes daily more grotesque. Its once green foliage continues to darken and shrivel. Besides this sight of decay, with its induced depression heightened by the silent, shadow filled building, the scent of death impresses on our nostrils. She roars: "Another day here and I'll go mad!"

"We'll soon be able to leave. I've found the course for Earth. There's the problem of time. We could reach Earth alive, although advanced in age."

"How long will the journey take?" Arrana gives an inquisitive scowl.

"By Kolaria time it will take thousands of years..."

"And you expect to survive that? We'd be old alright: dead! Lucirin, sometimes you make no sense at all."

I give her a smile. "I know it must seem strange to you, but time for us will not be the same as time in Kolaria. Because of the great distance travelling at great velocity, our time will shrink from what we would experience here. I don't expect you to understand it; just accept we'll survive the journey."

"You ask a lot. But you Aesir have strange ways. I remember the weird time change the Aesir used against us on Gahes."

"Oh yes, the time alteration field, used to neutralize gravity. It is opposite to what we need."

"And the hibernators?"

"They help to extend life. We'll have to use them if we want to reach Earth alive."

"But didn't you say that Heimbal's aliens came from afar, from another part of the sky? Why don't they die from old age?"

"They can slow the life processes and become perfectly mummified. Their science of distant space flight is much advanced over that of Aesiris."

Arrana becomes contemplative. She places a hand on her hip and leans against the computer console. "Don't tell me, let me guess. You want to return to Heras. You'd force the giants to give you that know-how. Well, count me out!"

"There's not much chance of forcing the giants into giving anything. But we do owe Heimbal a visit for his treachery, don't you think?"

After a thoughtful moment, she answers: "For that I'm with you."

The glow from our viewer's bubble is all the more eerie with the absence of our Arransin companions. We approach Heras cautiously.

"You seem nervous," Arrana observes.

"For good reason. Either the Aesir or Herasian fleet could greet us, and either could be fatal."

"That I know, for sure. But you seem more nervous than from the brood of capture."

"My worst fear is to be taken by Heimbal. He would yield us to his alien friends."

"Now that be indeed a tearful muse."

The surface of Heras comes into plain view, revealing that our fears were ill founded. Everything has been obliterated. Quareg and Tasis are reduced to rubble.

"Aesir. It fits what I told you about abandoning Kolaria. They made total war on Heimbal."

"But Aesir never behaved so vile..."

In flight over the Capitol we see wrecks of Herasian ships strewn over the flight port, the very ships we restored to full working order. They were caught by surprise, making this Herasian disaster difficult to understand. "This is how the Aesir gained the upper hand. With few or no ships to trouble them they had free reign."

"Everything gone...I don't believe this bubble..."

"What's puzzling is how the Herasians could be caught so off guard, unless - a *festival!* Those fools! I expressly prohibited the military participating in any such festivity."

"You forget the work of Heimbal in our leave."

Of course. He insisted that they attend the festivals to work his trance and win their full allegiance. The Aesir struck during an orgy, with impeccable timing thanks to Maiori, taking advantage of the Herasian weakness.

"Lucirin, we must go outside, to make sure."

I now see the total picture. After our Revolt the Aesir withdrew to build an invasion force, knowing they needed a five-to-one numerical offset against the alien 'blind'. They left behind on Aesiris only enough ships to protect the planet from lone bandits: us! Possessing a full psychological profile of Heimbal from ages past, they computed to happen exactly what did happen: his attempt to rid himself of us through betrayal. The fool, defeated by his pathological desire for control and underestimation of Aesir guile.

"My family, and the people I knew! They're...?" Arrana's voice trails.

"I'm afraid so. There's nothing left of Quareg."

"Take me to my brother's house. I'll find it."

We skim over the ruins of houses, shops and streets. Nothing stirs below except sheets of snow blowing between blackened ruins. Arrana finds the area where her brother's house had been, and prepares to disembark. At the portal I warn her of what she is going to find. She looks straight into my eyes, her forehead creased; she says nothing but dashes out to the ruined houses.

After some time she returns, shaking with trauma. She sits in silence on the deck against the ship's panelling, her knees drawn up and head lowered. The tragedy of our conflict has touched her personally, but she is too proud to openly display tears. I wait for her to speak.

"This is the greatest ruin in all our days," she says finally, "all because of us!" The thought appears to weigh heavily on her, and looking at me with her fierce eyes it is clear on whom she places most of the blame.

"This is unquestionably a tragedy, but I told you what to expect. We can't afford to be overcome with grief. Not now. We're here to find Heimbal."

"You're as heartless as any Aesir!" she explodes. "I expect nothing better from you, you who had a robot for a mother! Don't you comprehend? Quareg was my home. Everything I loved was here; now it's all swept away by those fanatic devils, and we're to blame. We pushed them to it!" She breaks down and sobs uncontrollably, her face in her hands to hide embarrassment.

"Instead of accusations, a closer look at the Capitol might... might be more productive."

A survey on foot of the Capitol's ruins confirms my theory. Under the annihilator scorched blocks and rubble from solar bombs are grisly remains of a festival occurring at the time of the strike. On one corpse is the tunic of a Herasian flight captain. "That explains how they were caught off guard." I motion into the space between fallen slabs. "I gave specific orders to the militia never to attend the festivals, for no reason other than to void...*this!*"

Arrana moves between two large stones: "There's still a trace of warmth. Their strike was not long ago, perhaps only days."

"Then Heimbal may not have fled yet if he survived. We'll need weapons and warm clothes from the ship, then we'll start looking for a stair passageway under this mess."

"For a...what?"

"A passage. To the aliens' hideout under the Capitol. Where they are, that's where we'll find Heimbal."

I recall the aliens' cave and roughly its access from my one and only meeting with those creatures, built far under the Capitol in a stone excavation that was likely preserved from the devastation on the surface. We dress warmly from the ship's provisions before sending 0-7-1 into flight as a precaution, for the aliens may have also invented an offset to its 'blind'. Then, armed with annihilator helmets and torches, we pick our way over the ruins.

A pile of rubble stretches the full length of the Capitol, that once magnificent building. Only the eastern wall is left intact. Its circular portal, the portal we entered on the evening of the Aesir festival, is perched high in the air, surrounded by a section of blackened wall. The immense social floor has collapsed to ground level, and lies buried under huge stones that comprised the building.

Guessing as best I can the route taken to the giants' compartment, we examine a depression amid the ruins where building stones have smashed through the underlying floor and through the planks of a platform beneath. Our weapons clear an opening large enough to squeeze between the stones and scorched wood, to confirm a passage under the platform. I encounter total darkness when I drop into the passage, and quickly shine my torch to relieve the moment's anxiety. Solid rock has been penetrated with a low tunnel bearing crude marks of Herasian workmanship. Steps lead into a well of night.

Arrana drops onto the torch-lit portion of stairs in my beam, the sound of her fall echoing from the depth below. We begin our descent with no little trepidation for the blackness we have entered, and I wonder in silence if this was the tunnel the Balam priests used to usher their victims into the alien giants' hands. I cannot think of any other reason for its construction.

The coolness of the air is scented by the damp rock encasing us. At sections the stairs become steep, where the rough stone of the tunnel roof can be touched at arm's length. Around every corner we breathe relief when our beams force shadows to retreat, revealing a safe descent until the next bend that remains shrouded in darkness. The sounds of our footsteps fill the tunnel. With Arrana in the lead, I look back to ensure that we are not followed. The steps behind trail upward in my torchlight and I think of the number we have already descended, dreading the necessity of a fast retreat.

At the base of the stairs, deep under the Capitol, we encounter a massive iron door with a bar on our side, to prevent exit. We swing the mass open; Arrana is the first to pass through. We enter a cave, where her torchlight illuminates two huge seats carved from solid stone. They look familiar.

"They sat in these? They're grand for sure!"

The stone cave swirls with moving contrasts of light and shadow from our torches. "This is where I met the aliens. They were sitting in those seats, looking down on me and not saying a word. It felt like I was on trial. They could've been reading my aura by natural ability, as they did with the Balam revellers from the festivals."

"What's this?" Arrana's torchlight, that had been bouncing around the chamber, fastens on a bench containing manacles and stains from spilled chemicals. Silhouettes of human figures, made from a powerful light source, discolor the bench.

"My guess is this is where the aliens stripped victims of their life auras."

A momentary silence sweeps my companion. She finally asks: "Those Herasians led off by priests during the frolics - they ended here? Then the aliens removed their life force. Is that what you mean, Lucirin?"

"Yes."

There is more silence, until her harsh voice pierces the blackness: "And you led me into this danger of such strange sciences! You knew about their crime upon Herasians, yet you did nothing to prevent it, and I think if we fall into their hands you'll treat me with the same callous disregard."

"Don't be silly. If there's danger I'm in it too, even more than you. Now lower your voice. You could attract real problems. Look at that..." My torch illuminates an immense doorway into the chamber at its opposite wall. Large enough to permit passage of the giants, its dimensions are staggering in their implications.

"They need one so big?" Arrana is awed by the suggested size of the creatures, whom she has never seen.

As we move toward the huge doorway a horrid stench assails us. Next to the door is a narrow tunnel, from where the foul odour emanates. "We should explore it," I tell her. "Their victims were left somewhere, so be prepared for an unpleasant sight."

Within moments of exploring the tunnel muffled groans exude from the darkness. We shine our torches into the inky depths of a natural cavern, and there, revealed in our beams, is a sight to shrivel my eyes: before us is the giants' human refuse of discarded revellers who had their life auras ripped from them. Once healthy and vital Herasians, they sit with twisted and shrunken bodies, their flesh melted from their bones, their skin of ashen hue and covered with sores. All are completely emaciated. One man has his face stuck to his shoulder; most have large patches of hair fallen from their scalps. All are too weak to stand but raise an arm to protest the light. A garbled murmur pervades the cavern. These are the most recent victims; throughout the cave are bones of victims long dead.

Our bursts put a quick end to their tormented existence.

One after another the deadly rays streak from our helmets, exploding on impact with our unfortunate targets. We reel from the fumes and are almost relieved to be back again in the giants' larger chamber. The discovery convinces me that the Aesir have not ended the last of Heimbal or his work.

"You make strange friends," Arrana protests. "I saw a lot of horror on Gahes, but nothing quite equalled *that!*"

With a new dread for the enemy we face, we proceed down a colossal corridor from the doorway, leading us deeper underground beyond the ruined city of Quareg on the surface. The light from our torches, reflecting down the corridor, eventually becomes lost in a distant hole of blackness indicating a lack of surface to repel our beams.

We douse the torches. A faint radiance ahead silhouettes the tunnel. A cavity of immense size beckons each cautious step, until we emerge into the mammoth void of an underground flight port. Burners, hanging at well spaced intervals along its curved walls, cast their glow into its expanse.

"Constructed for the alien ship!" I whisper.

"In all my days, I never dreamt anything like this be possible, not on Heras."

"Cut out of solid rock, by hand labor, bit by bit. It shows what even simple people can do when they have the determination."

"You say Herasians did this? Not those aliens?"

"You can see their workmanship in the stone. We could be surrounded by a whole network of hidden catacombs." I pause to gaze around the immense hollow. "It must have taken ages to excavate, using thousands of workers, right under Aesir noses."

Across the glossy floor are two massive iron doors. Tremendous in size, they are sufficient to allow a giant flight-ship through, but have been blasted open.

"They left in a hurry," Arrana motions.

"It's not difficult to guess what happened. The aliens were caught in their chamber under the Capitol with their victims on the night of the attack. They hurried down the tunnel to their ship but didn't wait to open the flight port doors to escape."

Half way around the floor from our position, opposite the giant ruined doors, a golden glow radiates from a large recess cut into the imposing wall. Arrana raises her hand in a gesture to listen. A barely audible, rhythmic sound is heard echoing in the cave, of human voices...*chanting!*

We skirt the wall of the flight port to finally look into the light-filled recess, to gaze upon an amphitheatre encircled by tiers of stone benches, each bench laboriously carved from the surrounding rock, stepped-fashion, and embellished with relief. Overhead, more sculpture depicts Heimbal in former days, worked into a domed roof ablaze in golden light.

"Herasians did this too?" Arrana's voice is subdued by the surprising skill of her people. The construction of the theatre, using primitive tools yet with such scale and beauty, was an enterprise that took the most zealous devotion. It brings home my Aesir learning that great Causes are the core of great cultures.

An imposing machine sits at the base of the recess: the *Balam 'altar'*. Next to it, a circle of clapping, chanting priests shuffle around an object on the floor. In their midst are two ornamented poles, a sedan, and on the sedan is a silver sphere. We must act quickly if I am to solve the enigma of Heimbal, for once the priests have their 'cabes-trebla' encased in its protective cylinder they can move with it through unseen tunnels, to become lost to me forever.

We charge down the amphitheatre, our weapons ready. The chanting abruptly stops. Among the priests is Eloez, whom I had not recognized under the hood of his cassock: "Lucirin!

The altar is sacred! It cannot be touched by one outside Balam!"

"Especially if the outsider is a cybernetics technician. When Heimbal reneges on his support I can't help losing reverence."

A priest in the crowd calls in a loud voice, holding his hands in the air: "Yea Heimbal, open the ground and swallow us all!"

"Your Heimbal is powerless with the 'cabes-trebla' disconnected from its console. I'm going to show you people, once and for all, how senseless are your beliefs. Heimbal is nothing more than a fiction projected into your minds by electronic wizardry."

I observe the silver sphere placed on the priests' carrier. Closer inspection confirms the need for a combination to split the casing without wreckage. Realizing the decision I am making, of whether to waste time trying to open it intact or expose the innards by smashing, a priest offers the combination. The sphere splits into two halves, revealing convolutions on its inner surface indicative of a cephalo-shield. As I remove the silver casing, in view of the priests who stare motionless at my effort, a transparent shell comes to light, filled with jelly. This is odd, since electronic circuits are not housed in that manner. Not until I remove the silver casing fully do I learn the true meaning of the 'cabes-trebla'. There, within the transparent shell, sitting in a jellied bath, is a living, human...*brain!*

"The b...brain of Heimbal!" I stutter in amazement, falling back in my hasty attempt to rise. The organ sits placidly under its transparent dome. A myriad of fine connectors trail from its bottom, barely visible in the reflected light. Arrana, too, is awed by the spectacle, but the priests remain motionless in silent protest. I look up to see their stone faces, etched in shadow, to encounter a dazzling sparkle dangling from a priest's hand.

It flickers off and on in rapid frequency, filling my eyes until my mind is saturated with its infernal glare. The priest drones: "You are powerless to resist." And so I am!

How long I remain in the trance I can only guess. There is the motion of bodies, the shuffle of feet and some confusion. When I awaken only the chief priest remains before us; the others have disappeared into the cavern's depths carrying their 'cabes-trebla'. Arrana also awakens, enraged, yet we have not been harmed nor even our weapons taken.

"You'll forgive us," the priest says, "but you cannot threaten our most sacred possession. I understand your thirst for revenge, and only hope you'll understand that what we did was for the better. We were all captives of the giants; it was always their will that prevailed."

"Don't throw your innocence at us. It was Heimbal in league with the giants who wanted to see our end on Aesiris, just as it is you, you priests, who are guilty of destroying Herasians in the most abominable way!"

"Our offerings to the giants were for peace. We of Balam, since we believe that pure and absolute happiness is the goal of human life, know that peace, of the mind and body, is the highest need for our lives. Without peace there be no happiness, without happiness there be no peace. When we submitted to the giants we followed the will of Heimbal, who ordered the sacrifices, but of folk who were shod with happiness, who went with eagerness, so we kept our oath to the cause of peace and happiness."

"Do you have any idea of what went on in the giants' chamber?"

"None. That was forbidden."

"Does Heimbal know?"

"Heimbal knows all in the way of peace and happiness."

Such simple fools, these Herasians, victimized by their own good natures and honest desire for human betterment, becoming prey to vampires from the far reaches of the galaxy through an unscrupulous leader willing to bargain with their lives, all because of their naive pursuit of peace and happiness.

"I must join the others," the priest continues. "For safety do not linger near the flight port. The giants are to return for our Illustrious One."

The giants to return! His statement wipes from my mind any further questions. Arrana too has the look of alarm. Our thoughts are now on 0-7-1. A fleeting glance back to the priest... He has already vanished.

Arrana and I return to the underground flight port to exit through the blasted doors at its far end. They open upon a windy ridge. I send a message for 0-7-1 and pass anxious moments waiting for our ship, hoping it will return first, not the alien vessel.

The wait gives time to reflect on recent events. What a mistake it was in thinking that Heimbal, as we knew him, was merely the mechanized memory of the Grand Master! Far from being a molecular transcript of that memory, the Balam 'alter' was a computer interfaced with the real thing. Upon reflection, why would the aliens go to the trouble of making a molecular transcript when they already had the original in Heimbal? Their control over the life processes could preserve a functioning human brain long after the decay of its physical body, and give it powers over an entire world. Such superior technology those creatures have over us! If the Aesir did not cut their plans short without doubt Heras would have become a full captive of Heimbal. Not only would its people be reduced to submission by hypnotic control, even the seismic nature of the planet would have been harnessed, as we saw on Degras. In the end,

all Heras would have been the physical extension of one corrupt and twisted mind, in the way that deeds of a human body
are the physical extension of a person's thought. More complete control over an entire world cannot be imagined. Such a
different scenario from the free society that, during the long
ages of Aesir domination, motivated Herasians in their struggle! What a scoundrel is Heimbal, to use people's genuine thirst
for self-expression to promote his own power lust and steal a
meaningful revolution! I put my faith in Heimbal, but when
people are unworthy of trust, when they are full of treachery
and deceit, the destruction that we see is inevitable. And such
betrayal by Maiori! If she had not informed the Veradi of my
plan to capture Aesiris, she would still be with me, millions of
people would still be alive, Aesiris and Heras would not have
been destroyed. I take no blame for what has happened; it was
not what I intended. The misfortune of Kolaria is due to the
mendacity of others.

Our wait ends. 0-7-1 appears without its 'blind' to show its
presence. On board, I waste no time to re-enter the cave and
blast the Balam 'altar'. It explodes violently. We exit from the
flight port and blast the roof of the area, causing a major collapse of rock upon its floor. More falling rock seals the entrance
before we escape into the Herasian night.

Days after our underground ordeal we continue to space
drift, relaxing and trying to make a decision on what should
be our next move. "Successful, aren't we?" Arrana complains.
"Aesiris and Heras in ruin, every colony in Kolaria a disaster.
There's only one place where we can return: Gahes! We belong
there after all!"

"You're forgetting there *is* another option," I remind her
from my position on a reposer, half opening my eyes to see her
reaction.

"Oh yes, the world that's so far we'd become old in our sleep reaching it. Some choice! The name is…"

"Earth. Don't dismiss it so lightly. To be certain, the prospect isn't the best, but consider the alternatives. There's no planet, moon or asteroid in all Kolaria where we can rest, where we'll not be sought by remaining Aesir star cruisers and loyal colonists who were dependent on Aesiris, and who must now be grieving its loss. In any place we settle in Kolaria we'll live in dread of being discovered, and will probably be discovered constantly, so we'll always be on the move. A good portion of our remaining lives will be used in hibernation anyway. Now what is better, that we spend time in hibernation going nowhere, or spend it in hibernation to a new destination? Speaking for myself, I've always found the boldest move pays unexpected rewards."

"You say the Aesir went to Ert…Earth. I hardly see much difference between here and where they are."

"The difference is: here we are hunted, there we wouldn't be. The Aesir were lords only in this part of the galaxy. By their Belief, worlds naturally teeming with life, like Gahes, are not controlled in the way most sterile worlds of Kolaria were. A world of natural life must be allowed its own order, meaning the Aesir on Earth would be defeated by their own philosophy. They would be self-condemned to remain insignificant and inconsequential instead of exercising dominion. We would be free of their tyranny even if they knew we were there, which they won't because they're not expecting us and I don't intend to announce our arrival."

"But I'm still a young woman! I want a full life, with fun and pleasure, not to spend my time in sleep! I'll never agree to throw away my life in hibernation!"

"I'm younger than you, Arrana."

"Then you're bent on self scathe!" Her voice rises to a sudden shrill. "For sure! You feel remorse for the ruin we brought on Kolaria, and especially on your beautiful Aesiris. You feel there be amends, that we receive the scourge."

"Don't be silly. It's merely the least evil we can cause ourselves to survive. But very well, *you* decide on a suitable world for our habitation."

And so we journey from one colony to another, only to find the desolation or danger I predicted. We cannot obtain solid fuel and must resort to the time consuming method of re-energizing 0-7-1 from solar radiation. During a fuel run, cruising in orbit around Kol, we are ambushed by star-cruisers whose attack we only escape by using the 'blind'. By appearances, their sole mission was to hunt us down. I use the occasion to press again for acceptance of Earth as our destination. This time there is no heated debate. Arrana has become resigned to Earth.

Preparations are made for the epic voyage. 0-7-1 is fully energized, nourishment is materialized and our hibernator reservoirs enlarged. Finally we are ready, and meet in the encapsulation compartment.

"It's like facing death!" Arrana sobs. She lies in her hibernator under an open canopy, her eyes staring through a layer of tears. "Lucirin, do you think this be our scourge?"

"Of course not."

"Strange, I say, we go to a world where the Aesir already are, as if we need them too. It reminds me of a rule they taught on Heras: 'Even evil needs goodness to grow'. Can that be true?"

"Possibly. But it has nothing to do with us."

There is a long silence as our attention is focused on ourselves, on our youthful strength, vigor and beauty. We shall not see ourselves like this again.

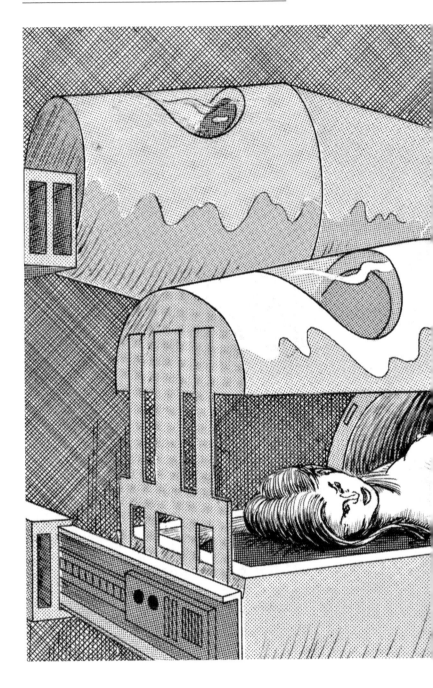

16

EARTH

MILLENNIA OF KOLARIA time have passed. Through them all, we slept. Reviving for periodic maintenance throughout the journey, I took the occasions, on her insistence, to awaken Arrana. On each awakening we spent periods immersed in the joy of living, feeling the delights of simple, physical existence, but with each revival the decision had to be made to return to the pods. Arrana's repugnance against such lengthy hibernation never waned. "It's only that we're in the middle of nowhere that forces me back," she would say. "My life is measured in days." Living life in such short stages heightens awareness of aging. Each awakening brought recognition of time's toll: slower reactions, loss of agility, fatigue, until this day of arrival on Earth when we display the wrinkled features and greying hair of people who have their lives behind them.

"The sky is so different on this world, Lucirin, don't you think?" Arrana's feet shuffle over dry soil, raising small dispersions of dust that catch the lights of our star cruiser under the night sky. She has her arms folded, her shoulders bent against the cold as she explores a small region in the lights of the ship. This area of the planet has a resemblance to Heras: dry and cool, being located at a high altitude.

I hand her a warm cape from the ship's wardrobe and join her to enjoy the Earth night. "I'm surprised by this world of our origin. As Aesir youths we were told that it was immensely cold, covered in sheets of ice, with people of brutish nature. Instead, we find warm regions, like Aesiris, and evolved humans like ourselves. Our descendants will find the Earth populations to be a rich source of compatible genetic material."

"Descendants?" Arrana laughs. "You think this old body can give new life? And let's not forget that little cut the Veradi did on you for your stay on Gahes. Your head must be still in hibernation."

"You mean the vasectomy. Ah yes, but you underestimate the technology at our disposal, as usual. New life doesn't have to come in the natural Herasian fashion. There were other ways known to the Aesir. Give me time to build incubators and before the end of an Earth year we'll have new life among us."

"It's not just a physical matter. Infants need caring, nursing. We're too old. In a few short years we'll pass on and leave them to themselves."

"That's why I'm delighted by this world. The people will be nursemaids to our descendants. They shouldn't find that displeasing, since I suspect we'll become part of their hierarchy."

My hope is soon realized. After days of remaining unseen, the Earth people approach cautiously, carrying baskets of strange foods. Numbering in the hundreds, they kneel and present their gifts with lowered heads. One woman, followed by her entourage, all on their knees, raises a bowl to Arrana. None dare look us in the face.

Later that evening while enjoying the food, sitting in 0-7-1's spacious dining area, Arrana smirks: "I never thought to be so gloried. All this kneeling and bowing is enough to give swelled pride."

I remind her: "Herasians thought Heimbal was god-like too, because he possessed advanced technology, and look what happened to him. We would do well not to become so conceited. But we can use the subservience of these people to collect information and learn their language."

"And how would you do that?"

"By our on-board memory transcriber. All we need is to converse with them and have them respond in their tongue, using the transcriber. We can have a working knowledge of their language in days, but we can't have them on board our ship. That will have to remain off-limits, so we'll have to remove the transcriber to their leader's house. This is supposing they cooperate. I'm certain they will, especially when I show the chief how he can be the beneficiary of our energy-materializer, or the victim of a death helmet. A threat and reward approach."

"That sounds easy enough. But you say you want our descendants. That's the trick I'd like to see."

"Give me time. It was a pretty standard procedure on Aesiris. We'll build incubators and keep the fetuses inside the ship. Earth people must never see them. I fear if they did they would consider us unusual beyond words."

"That's true, for sure. I consider it quite unusual myself."

A year of the planet passes, with events unfolding as foreseen, until one day we encounter an excited group of people giving startling news: another 'ship from the sun,' in their words, has come, carrying two passengers of giant stature who extract a tribute in human life. I am numbed by the thought of the giant aliens following us to this world. The crushing defeat of Heras meant they had to search again for victims, and by returning to Heras we stumbled into their picture at an opportune time for them. Following behind us, using their 'blind,' they traced our trajectory during the full flight to Earth. Still, we must be certain. The people's account does not wholly fit the description of aliens familiar to us, for they describe beings of violent nature and destructive habits, whereas on Heras the aliens were docile, always remaining unseen.

We visit the areas where the giants are provoking terror, and witness the fearful servitude instilled into the people, without once setting eyes on the creatures ourselves.

"They could be hiding behind their 'blind,'" I mention when observing one horror-stricken village. Men and women sit helplessly outside their homes, weeping and wailing. The aliens concentrated on the youth of the village for abduction. "There's no reason it couldn't shield an individual as well as a ship."

"The Earth people say they come and go. Perhaps they raids the whole planet."

"That's very probable. After their long mummification during their flight they must be 'hungry' for new life. I'm convinced they're the same aliens we knew on Heras, the very same ones, although their method of operation is different. Quite possibly we're seeing the value Heimbal played in their scheme: the role of swineherd, to keep victims under control until ripe for slaughter."

"Then they're no longer in league with Heimbal?"

"I guess not, which means that we and they need not come into direct confrontation."

I resolve that belligerence toward the giants would cause unnecessary risk to ourselves, and decide to leave them to their nefarious practices. Then, one day when Arrana and I are guests in the house of the clan chief, there occurs an explosion that shakes the stone structure as if from an earth tremor. We rush outside to see a column of black smoke rising from where 0-7-1 had been stationed. Hovering high overhead is an *Aesir* vul-canae! The sight grips me with anger and fear. To lose our flight-ship, a ship that saved our lives, that nursed us in our journey to Earth, that became a friend and member of our company, and without which we are now imprisoned by gravity on this world, gives grief to our aged hearts. Feeling all this, and saying nothing, we stand in shocked silence in front of the chief's house, waiting the approach of the enemy star-cruiser.

The wait is not long. Young people, much younger than I thought possible, and not just Aesir, approach us to escort us into their vessel. These cannot be the same people who left Aesiris, and I realize the migrants must also have undertaken a breeding program with the Earth inhabitants, years before our landing. Arrana and I are quickly identified without difficulty and these strange men forcibly escort us into their vessel, to an interrogation room where we face several officers.

"Is it your practice to annihilate vul-canae without provocation?" I demand, shaking with indignation.

"Calm yourself, old man," one of the figures responds in the icy Aesir manner. "First introductions. I am Captain Koptin, and you are the infamous Lucirin, twenty-nine Andra-naudae, master criminal, responsible for the destruction of Aesiris and its dependents that formed the most advanced civilization in its galactic sector, of which my progenitors belonged. We find your anger to the destruction of your star-cruiser, which you say was 'without provocation,' ironic, to say the least."

"How long have you been here?"

"We've been on Earth one generation, longer than you, which raises a better question: How did you enter Earth space without detection? By using the alien 'blind'?"

"Yes."

"Then you have been in partnership with the alien giants, to ravage the inhabitants of Earth."

"No! We have not!" I am alarmed by Koptin's allegation, for I remember well the justice of Aesiris. If these men think we are the aliens' accomplices it will mean our executions.

"We learned of the 'blind' while on Heras. The giants followed us to Earth. It was a surprise for us to learn of their presence here."

"That can be verified from your Earth friends," Koptin replies, and motions an aide to do the chore. "As long as we share your company I would like to hear your account of the events preceding your arrival here, and particularly your description of your home planet. I have never had the opportunity to speak with a living person who saw Aesiris with his own eyes, even if he was the one who destroyed it."

Koptin offers us two seats in the ship's compact but comfortable discussion chamber, and suggests that we drink with him an Earth tea while I give my account. He is not lacking in courtesy, again typical for an Aesir. My voice is even as I tell the events that resulted in our flight to Earth, describing with much less sentiment than I might have thought the planet of my birth. Koptin asks few questions throughout my discourse; I assume I am being recorded and he probably sees no reason to clutter that record with his own voice.

"How did you find us?" I ask.

"By the usual cephalo-probe. But we wouldn't have even thought of looking for you had it not been for the alien giants spreading their terror around the planet. We knew who they were and where they came from, which could mean they had a helping hand in finding Earth. That is why we came looking for Aesir or Herasians in our old cephalo files, with you, in particular, in mind. It's a cleaning up operation, you might say, after the giants were removed."

"Then the giants are finished?" Arrana asks.

"Yes, they are. We sent their carcasses and infernal machines plummeting into the sun not thirty days ago. We don't want any evidence of their existence to remain on Earth. In case you're interested, they were captured because of their drunkenness."

Our puzzled expressions solicit Koptin to explain: "Nitrogen narcosis. The aliens were not adapted to the high concentration of nitrogen at Earth's atmospheric pressure. It caused them to be drunk and behave wildly, revealing their inward, criminal natures. If it weren't for such induced irrationality they would have been very illusive with that shielding of theirs. By the way, we have it now. That's why we weren't detected by your ship."

Anger returns to my face, which provokes Koptin to continue: "Yes, it was a pity to annihilate such a star-cruiser. You realize that it had to be done, since I'm sure the ship was imprinted to your service and would have destroyed us on first notice."

"Would it not have been possible to call a truce between us? After all, we are advanced in age and couldn't possibly threaten you. And even if the blood still ran hot in our veins, this is Earth, not Aesiris. You can have no mission here like you had there."

"A worthy point regarding Earth," Koptin says, rising from his seat with the excitement of debate, "and Earth it should remain, not a mockery of development fitted to suit your idealized and purely materialistic notions. We do not look with favor on your giving these people your devices. Regarding our not having a mission here, you couldn't be more wrong. You see, the Aesir Empire was a complex structure that went far beyond anything the Tsia ever expected, and like all such growing structures it was approaching chaos. This truth became increasingly clear to the more enlightened Veradi in the last years. They realized that the chances of survival for their whole civilization were mounting against them as time went on, and that one day, in all probability, a radical element would occur that would cause the collapse of everything they had built. That radical was you two: combinations of genes and circumstances thrown up by nature to eradicate a cancer from the natural cosmos. Perhaps you have always considered yourself an unusually lucky person, Lucirin, undoubtedly you have been, and for good reason, you have always had a powerful ally in the probability laws that govern our universe.

"Now with Earth it is different. Here *you* are out of place; we have learned our lesson, so the new Aesiris will be part-and-parcel of a more organic whole, more in place with a totally integrated complexity. Oh yes, the Earth inhabitants will advance. They will advance according to the development plan we have set for them, which, of course, will always aim toward that final goal of a harmonious world order ruled by the tenets of our one and only Belief. Our mission today and for thousands of years to come is to prepare Earthlings for our doctrine, both biologically and culturally, since like Herasians without that preparation they cannot live up to it fully. Thus, throughout future ages civilizations will rise and fall, there will be peace and war, ages of plenty and ages of scarcity, and behind it all we shall be present. We shall raise whole movements of people and propel them in predestined directions, even against our interests so in the end we can destroy unwholesome ideas that would be an impediment to our Belief if it is to have effect. There will not be a great person in human history, whether in government or science, who will not have a shadow figure at his or her elbow, to guide, to instruct the powerful and clever into new paths of conduct and thought. Those paths may or may not have their supposed purpose of the time; what is certain is that each will be another thread in the weave of a new Aesiris on Earth."

I listen to Koptin in stunned disbelief. *A new Aesiris on Earth,* planned now for millennia to come, and manipulated into existence by a secret sect of fanatics that will remain unknown to Earth's inhabitants until that fatal day when the age of tyranny is sprung. For certain, here is a new twist to Aesir perversion I had not considered. They do not wish to enforce their own rule from above, true, instead they will manipulate a planet's history from below, to have it *grow* into the form they set, becoming itself the new Aesiris. In my private thoughts I decide that somehow the Earth inhabitants must be warned.

The aide sent outside, who was to verify from the people that we were not in association with the aliens, returns. Koptin appears pleased and resumes speaking: "We'll not detain you longer. You're free to live out the remainder of your lives here with your Earth friends. We see, Lucirin, you have started, luckily as yet not fully rooted, another advancement program like the one you began on Heras for those inhabitants, with such drastic consequences. With the destruction of your flight-ship and technical gadgetry those activities have been cut short. In any case, no matter. Our computations show that any advancement you produce here will have little genuine effect on the general course of Earth's history. It is in the warm regions of the opposite hemisphere where the greatest concentrations of Earth's population reside."

He motions us back to the ship's portal, then steps outside for a first hand look at the terrain we have chosen. "We've picked Earth conditions reminiscent of our home worlds, which makes me wonder just how Earth-prone we really are. You Herasians have chosen a cold land, and we Aesir a warm one."

He turns back toward his ship, leaving us standing in the cool, open air. The Earthling chief and his family come to meet us, joining us in a group as we watch the Aesir vul-canae levitate and disappear over the eastern horizon.

An explosion of chatter breaks out among the Earth people. Arrana turns a worried glance: "Without 0-7-1 we have no home."

"We're also without transportation," I add.

We examine the ground where 0-7-1 last stood, in hope of salvaging some of its parts. Nothing is left; only a smouldering crater surrounded by jabbering Earthlings.

"Arrana! We shall yet foil the Aesir's mad schemes!" My wild assertion brings a look of mild sympathy to the downcast face of my aging companion. She does not take me seriously. "We'll warn Earth's future inhabitants of the danger that lurks for them. We still have the memory transcriber that we removed from 0-7-1 to learn our friends' language and culture. It will endure for millennia. We must embark on a project that will occupy all our energies during these last years of our lives."

"What of your other ambitions? Don't you want to teach the Earth people in our ways, to give our sons and daughters the gift of Aesir knowledge?"

"There's not much point in elevating people materially if we abandon them to the despotism of a fanatic sect. No! More important is our continued struggle with the Aesir menace."

Two and a half years of this planet pass since our meeting with Koptin. Arrana is dead, from an aneurism. I continue work with help from the Earth people on the last details of the cephalo-shield for the transcriber. The transcriber sits here, in this stone room of the chief's house. I must yet place the memories of my life into its molecules and transfer the machine to its hiding place.

And so the story of my life has been told, future one. We have returned full circle to the beginning. It is here where the account of my experiences began. You now possess knowledge of what has happened in the past. Use that knowledge wisely in your time. Do not minimize the Aesir threat. Warn your populations. If you do not, your descendants are certain to fall victims to a world despotism that in its extent will recognize no bounds, that in its zeal will tolerate no freedom of the will.

"I think it's ended, he's moving his hands," the youthful blond man shouted to his friends. The three scurried to the porthole to also look upon the prostrate figure. A plump Bolivian climbed nervously through the porthole, making as much haste as he could to examine the frail form. Four pairs of eyes peered watchfully from above.

"Thees mon is verry tire-ed," the Bolivian said, looking up at the four. "I theenk eet wud be best if he go to 'ospital. Bot don't worry, he weell be OK"

Two days later Doctor Niemeyer was allowed to tell the story to his associates, Boyd, Ryan and the two Jennings, who sat attentively around the old metal bedstead in a private room of the town hospital. The doctor rested with two oversized pillows propped behind his back while he narrated the account, becoming visibly more tired as the story progressed. The stimuli of his recent memories provoked renewed fears and anxieties. "There's some moments I would like to forget," he said. "If it were me in those real life situations I would have given up. I'm certainly not as strong an individual as was Lucirin, and not so criminally vindictive. Perhaps that's why this has been such a trying experience. But I wouldn't have missed it for the world."

Doctor Niemeyer's head sunk into the thick pillows, his eyes closed in sleep. A nurse from the hospital motioned to the four guests that the interview was ended.

"If only they would let me take recordings of his sleep talk!"

Mark Jennings exclaimed as they walked down the hallway of the hospital. "I'm sure we're missing a gold mine in words and phrases that could help identify the language association of those people."

"It *is* lamentable," Ryan responded. "We're going to need all the help we can get."

Boyd caught the despairing note in Ryan's voice. "Why the sad look, Charlie? This is the break we've been needing for a long time. We now have evidence supporting the doctor's theory. The academic profession will have to take notice."

"We're not just dealing with a scientific theory any more," Ryan said. "We're dealing with a serious threat to our world, one that's been in place for a very long time. If history has been manipulated and our societies are controlled, it means that our world is not free. But I confess, I don't see much that we can do."

Boyd responded: "We first have to get the doctor's story known...and accepted."

The four walked to the parked jeep outside the hospital. Ryan placed a hand on the vehicle and turned to Boyd: "Have you seen the dome in the last two days?"

"Only the exterior. I've been busy with the doctor's affairs and some paperwork around camp."

"Well, the 'sarcophagus' has liquefied. There's nothing left of it. Even the light inside the dome is out. It's now as black as night inside. The whole energy package of that machine is gone, and with it everything that made it of value to us. The tiara has been stolen, most likely by our camp help for its silver, and I'm even afraid that when some reputable professor or whoever gets around to examining our claim, the shell itself will be gone. Just yesterday a prospector was looking it over. The value of scrap copper isn't lost on such people. In the end we'll have no tangible evidence of our stupendous find left, the kind that established people of learning are so insistent upon."

"There's the doctor's account," Leslie asserted. "Surely people wouldn't believe he made up the whole story, especially when it's been such an emotional experience for him."

"That's exactly what they will believe," Ryan assured. "The doctor is already known for his unorthodox views, and is considered somewhat of an eccentric. If he reports this find without tangible proof he'll be suspected of fabricating a story to justify his outlandish theory. If he persists he will only convince people that he's sincere, but laboring under a delusion and in need of psychiatric help. We can be of no real benefit because none of us has experienced the dream, meaning that with our own enthusiasm we could be too credulous in accepting his account. In all, a cloud of doubt is cast over our find, which will simply be mentioned as another of those 'uncertainties' that plague this science." Ryan braced himself against the jeep, folded his arms and crossed one leg over the other. He could see that his own pessimism had taken effect on his three partners.

"There must be *something* we can do," Boyd insisted.

"If you believe that, you're caught in a paradox. You believe the doctor's story, don't you?"

"Most certainly! Every word of it!"

"Then you must believe what was told us about the Aesir sect to be true. If our world is manipulated there really isn't much hope of ever convincing anyone with a measure of prestige or authority. Come to think of it, that could be the reason for the doctor's lack of success in the first place: his theory is dangerous."

Silence hung over the small group with Ryan's last words, the feelings of delight and exuberance of the preceding days given way to discouragement. Ryan slapped the jeep's hood and moved into the driver's seat. The others drove with him through the town to the open, dusty plain. Overhead sprawled an endless expanse of deep blue sky.

"The doctor is back at the beginning," Ryan said, raising his voice to be heard over the noise of the vehicle. "He is and will remain a scientific outcast, with as much support for his theory as if the dome had never been discovered."